Also by Yawatta Hosby

One By One
Something's Amiss
Twisted Obsession
Six Plus One
Perfect Little Murder
Two Book Boxset
Urban Legends

Watch for more at yawattahosbysbooks.wordp.

Copyright Page

Dedication

To my beautiful grandmothers, Elsie and Olivia. I miss you so much.

Acknowledgments

I would like to thank my first critique partners Chase and Anam. Even though you guys didn't stick with me until the end of my novella, you taught me a lot. You gave me the confidence to show my fiction to other people for objective feedback.

I'd also like to thank Kathleen and Melissa, who were my critique partners/beta-readers. Kathleen taught me how to write sensual sex scenes without sounding vulgar, and Melissa taught me how to delete scenes that aren't necessary in moving the story along. Thank you for believing in *Something's Amiss* and encouraging me to publish it. I'd been messing with the story since 2011!

I'd like to thank James (www.goonwrite.com) for designing the cover. Thank you for taking a chance on a new author.

I'd also like to thank my very first Creative Writing class. Nettie, Melissa, Robin, Chuck, Pat, Lyle, Larry, Jan, Jon, and Anne, you guys rock! I loved spending time with you and getting a chance to read your raw talent. It was fun watching your different writing styles develop throughout the ten weeks. I still can't believe it's been over a year! Thank you for believing in me and motivating me to follow my dreams.

And last but not least, I'd like to say thank you to Melissa again. She's been an amazing writing buddy, and I hope we continue to have our mini-adventures. She agreed to be my editor for this novella. Thank you for your line-by-line edit and your honesty. I hope one day I can repay you.

Chapter One

Oliver stood in front of his apartment door. His key was stuck. Instead of calmly turning it like usual, he yanked it out of the knob, causing the metal to almost bend. He rubbed his eyes. He opened the door, and threw his mail on the end table, then slumped onto his leather couch.

Oliver stared in front of him into complete darkness. He reached for the answering machine and pushed the button to hear his messages.

"Honey, I'm calling to see if you want Chinese instead of Italian tonight. Well, call me when you get this message, or it'll just be a surprise. Doesn't matter where we go as long as I'm with you. Love you, Honey."

Beep.

"Hey, Honey, it's Kate. Where are you? You're not answering your door or your phone. Call me when you get this."

Beep.

"Honey, it's not like you to cancel plans and not let me know what's up. You need to call me and let me know where you are. And it better be soon!"

Beep.

Oliver rubbed his eyes again.

"Honey, it's late. Where are you? Sorry about being mad earlier. Please call me to let me know you're okay... I'm getting worried. This is your lovely, beautiful girlfriend, Kate. Call me; I don't care what time it is."

Beep.

Sighing, Oliver stood and walked toward the hallway, his eyes fully adjusted to the dark. He entered his bedroom, kicked off his sneakers, and flopped on the bed.

He was not all right. There was only one person who could make him feel better. Oliver looked at his alarm clock: 3:30. The red numbers provided the only light in the room. He took his cell phone out of his pocket and dialed a number he knew by heart.

POE LAY NEXT TO LEO in bed. Awakened by her ringing cell phone, she yawned, then stumbled toward the dresser, stubbing her toe on the corner of her bed frame. She shrieked in agony. She covered her mouth and gritted her teeth. "Hello? Hello?" she said into the phone.

"I'm sorry I called so late, Poe."

Is my ex really calling at this hour? Oliver hadn't tried to contact her ever since she moved back to Pittsburgh. Poe had wanted to remain friends but gave up when he wouldn't return her calls or emails.

She glanced over at Leo sleeping, then tiptoed out of her bedroom and into the living room. She tripped over the couch, hurting her big toe again. Poe reached to rub her foot and fell on the couch. "Oliver?"

"Poe, I'm sorry for calling late. I'm sorry."

"What's wrong?" She took a deep breath, anticipating his answer. Oliver sounded so distraught that she didn't know if she could handle what he had to say.

He hesitated. "Jenna's dead."

Poe gasped. She pulled her shirt away from her neck; she felt suffocated. Heat rushed through her body. This could not be happening. It had to be a joke.

"She got hit by a car on the sidewalk. By the time I made it to the emergency room, everyone already heard the news that she was gone."

No way. Jenna was coaching Oliver on what to say. In a few seconds, Poe would hear laughter, then everything could go back to normal.

"I can't believe it; we just talked this morning." Oliver took a deep breath. "Poe, are you still there?"

She whispered, "Yes, I'm here. Oh my god, I can't believe it. I'm so sorry. Are you okay?"

"...It's still a shock. Will you be okay?"

Of course not. This news was too much to handle. How could this be? "Yes...I'm sorry. I have to go."

"Call me if you need anything."

Poe swallowed a knot in her throat. It hurt so much that she couldn't respond. She hung up the phone and sat in silence, letting the news sink in. She wished she was dreaming.

Reaching her bedroom, Poe lay down and leaned towards Leo. She nudged him but he didn't budge. She curled against his body that was warm, but otherwise lay like a corpse.

Corpse—like Jenna.

Tears ran down her face. She tasted the salty rainfall. "Leo, wake up."

He grunted.

Poe shook him until he turned over. "LEO, WAKE UP!"

He opened his eyes. "Babe, what's wrong?"

"I have to go to Rhode Island." She wiped her eyes.

Leo jerked up and frowned. "Are you breaking up with me?"

"My best friend died tonight."

"I'm so sorry, Babe." He pulled Poe towards him, enveloping her into his arms. "What can I do to help?"

Chapter Two

That morning, Poe boarded her flight at 11:26 AM and arrived at the T.F. Green Airport in Warwick around 1 PM. After collecting her heavy suitcases, she texted her sister, Keisha, to let her know that she made it to her destination.

She didn't know how she should act in front of her ex. They were strangers now. She didn't come to Rhode Island to create drama or complicate his life. It wasn't her intention to win Oliver back. No. Poe came to mourn the loss of her best friend and to attend the funeral.

She walked towards the sliding front doors, catching a glimpse of Oliver through the glass. He tugged at his shirt, readjusted his hat, and pulled at his ear. Poe stopped in the middle of the lobby, which was a mistake. A crowd ran into her, pushing her forward, like a bunch of fans trying to approach a celebrity.

Outside, they met each other's gazes. A smile stretched across Oliver's lips. He strolled towards her. "Hey."

"Hey." Poe looked into his deep blue eyes. There was something in those eyes that always distracted her from her surroundings. Quickly, she looked down at his chest. "I like your shirt." The gray v-neck brought out Oliver's eyes and black curly hair.

"It was always your favorite." He rubbed the back of his neck. "Sorry we haven't spoken in so long, and the first time we do, I have to give you bad news."

Poe shook her head; she forced back tears, afraid of breaking down. *Oliver shouldn't see me vulnerable. It's not his responsibility anymore.* Avoiding eye contact, she said, "I'm just happy you called."

Oliver hugged her. The warmth of his body soothed her even though she was reluctant to admit it. He could only be a friend now. He rubbed his palm over her back. "Let me carry your bags." His warm breath brought her back to the present. There was no point standing around a crowded airport, where people kept bumping and running into them. Those people were in a hurry, but Oliver and Poe were at a standstill. The next few days would be tough. Poe didn't know if she was mentally prepared.

Oliver grabbed her luggage while Poe held on to her purse. Without any effort, Oliver carried them to the parking lot; Poe followed, admiring his strength. Once they reached his blue Jetta, he popped the trunk. She stood behind him. To end the awkward silence, she said "You didn't have to pick me up."

"I wanted to. Did you not want me to come?" He slammed the trunk down and turned to face her.

She bit her bottom lip. "I didn't say that." She didn't know the right things to say. She knew Oliver would be sensitive to whatever she said.

Poe held her breath when Oliver stared at her for a long second. His jaw tensed, and his eyes darkened. Agonizing silence lingered between them, heightening her nervousness. Poe dropped her gaze and stepped to the car door.

It's going to be a long ride to Providence.

Before she could touch the handle, Oliver opened the passenger door. Whether mad or not, people could count on him to be a gentleman. She got in the passenger seat and sighed.

Was it always this awkward when people met their exes?

Oliver took long strides around the car, then slid in the driver's seat. He quickly put the key in the ignition as if avoiding her, but he didn't start the engine. His hands remained on the steering wheel. He inhaled a deep breath, leaning into his seat. With his head tilted, he stared into Poe's eyes. He didn't say a word.

Poe looked out the windshield. Gray clouds blocked the sun, causing dimness to the atmosphere. There were a couple of scratches on the dashboard, and some dust coated the air vents.

"When's the funeral?" Poe asked.

"I don't know yet."

"How you holding up?"

"I can't believe she's gone. It's like...I'm in a dream and haven't woken up yet." He frowned. "Know what I mean?"

Poe nodded.

Oliver squeezed her arm. "How are you holding up?"

"I don't know. She was too young to die." Poe fidgeted with her hands. "God, I'm using past tense already. This sucks."

Oliver squeezed her hand. "It means a lot that you came."

Eventually, they drove off; the radio played on low volume, filling in the silence. They reached Providence, passing a Holiday Inn on the left side of the road. Poe turned to Oliver, bewildered. "You just passed a hotel."

He shrugged his shoulders. "So?"

"I need to check in."

"I'm not letting you stay in a hotel."

"Well, it's not like I'm going to stay with you." Poe didn't meet his gaze. She wasn't kidding herself. She had a boyfriend back home, and Oliver had clearly moved on with his new girlfriend. It stung a little, but it was something she had to get over. "How's Kate?"

"You know about her?"

"Just because we didn't keep in touch doesn't mean I haven't heard about your life through Jenna and Dominic."

Jenna, his cousin, was the queen of gossip. She had meddled in people's lives, thinking she knew best. It was an addiction. Since Poe liked guidance, they made a good team.

Oliver smirked. "Well then, how's Leo?"

Poe glanced at him with a questioning look.

"Jenna and Dominic," he answered.

She sighed. "Leo wanted to come with me for support, I guess."

"Why didn't he?"

"I asked him not to."

He raised an eyebrow. "Kate doesn't even know yet. You were the only person I wanted to talk to about it."

He had called me, not Kate. Should I be happy about that?

Oliver tensed, clearing his throat. "I'm not letting you stay in a hotel. You'll stay with my mom."

"I don't want to be a burden."

"Yeah right. She thinks of you as a daughter."

Poe loved Lily MacNamara. Lily had accepted Poe as her son's girlfriend, no questions asked. If Poe would've played her cards right, she could have been her daughter-in-law by now. But no, she did what she did best. She sabotaged the relationship because she got scared.

Shaking her head, Poe looked out of the window. Families sat out on their porches, and kids played on the sidewalk in this humid summer day. Oliver pulled over along the curb in front of his mom's house. It was a green two-story home with white shutters; it looked odd compared to all the brick homes on the block in the Irish neighborhood of Smith Hill.

Oliver got out of the car and grabbed Poe's suitcases. She followed him silently to the front door. He let her in with his key. "I'll see you later?"

"If you want."

"Do you want me to?"

"Yeah." Poe smiled.

OLIVER DECIDED HE WOULD take a nap once he reached the apartment. He hadn't slept, and he knew very well the reason for it. Now that Poe was in town, he intended to spend most of his time with her since he didn't know when she'd be leaving.

Oliver leaned against the elevator wall. Poe had looked ravishing in her skinny jeans and turquoise t-shirt. The aroma of her Tommy Girl perfume still teased his senses. She hadn't changed a bit. She was exceptionally beautiful. Her lips had quivered when she spoke, and she avoided eye contact with him, attempting to hide her feelings. But he knew Poe well enough to not be fooled.

Oliver stepped off the elevator and found Kate pacing back and forth in front of his door. He sighed. *Guess I won't get any sleep now.* She saw him and stopped pacing. She ran towards him with her hand over her heart. "I'm so sorry, Honey." She hugged him.

"For what?" Oliver pulled away and crossed to his door.

"When you didn't call me last night, I was concerned and called Dominic this morning. He told me about Jenna." She smiled weakly. "I'm just happy to see you here in one piece."

The key stuck again, but Oliver managed to open his door on the first try. He let Kate go inside his apartment first; he shut the door behind them.

"Where have you been? I've been waiting in the hallway for at least an hour, which I wouldn't have to do if I had a key."

Oliver had begun the relationship with Kate as a rebound, but then he started to care for her. On paper, Kate was perfect for him because she wanted kids and marriage. She didn't get scared when things got serious, and she liked to talk about her feelings, but Oliver's heart wasn't in it. He went through the motions because he was lonely. "You want a key. I'll give you a key," he said dismissively.

"I want you to *want* to give me a key."

"I don't mind doing that; you're always here anyway."

Kate kissed Oliver on the cheek. "So where were you?"

He knew she wouldn't like what he had to say, but he didn't believe in lying to avoid a headache or argument. "I went to the airport to pick up Poe."

"Poe...as in your ex?" She placed her hands on her hips, frowning. "As in the one your mother always talks about in front of me, letting me know she feels I'm not good enough?"

Oliver sighed. "Not now, I just lost my cousin, someone I was close to. Please not now." He sat, slumping on the couch.

"I'm sorry."

Oliver grabbed Kate by her hand and pulled her closer to him. She rested her head on his chest as he circled his arms around her. "So you talked to Dominic. How did he sound?"

"How would you sound if you lost your wife?"

Devastated. Just losing Poe a year ago was rough. He couldn't imagine never talking to her, never getting to touch her, and never getting to see her again. Poe wasn't his wife or fiancé, but he had wanted to marry her. Those feelings would never change, and it hurt Oliver that Poe didn't want the same thing.

"I need to see him. Want to come?" Oliver asked.

Chapter Three

K nock. Knock.

When Dominic saw Poe standing at the door, his eyes widened and a weak smile stretched on his lips. He resembled a younger version of Antonio Banderas. "What are you doing here?"

"Oliver didn't know when the funeral was, so I took the earliest flight just in case. My boss is pretty understanding. It helps that I'm dating his son." Poe grinned and followed Dominic inside the house.

"Ah, it's dating now. Last I heard, he was just a fuck buddy."

"He is." She shrugged, sliding her hands in her jean pockets. "But he wants to be more." It was awkward engaging in girl talk with him without Jenna. Usually he would tease them. Now, Dominic looked like he could break down any moment. His hair was a hot mess, one side flat and the other side wild dark brown wavy strands dancing to a unique beat. There were bags under his eyes. His bottom lip trembled. Dominic cried the kind of hysterical cry where you shake and can hardly swallow; the kind where if you stop, you may throw up.

Poe hugged him. "I'm so sorry for your loss."

"She was here...just yesterday. What am I going to do without her, Poe? I can't live without her."

Not knowing what to say, Poe rubbed Dominic's back gently. She squeezed his hand, crossing to the kitchen, forcing back tears. Dishes were piled up in the sink. Old food was left on the counter. She made coffee while he sat in a chair, sobbing. She placed his coffee mug in front of him and sat on a chair facing him.

"I have all these things I have to do. I have to plan the funeral, plan the wake, talk to the funeral home, and talk to my lawyer about My Love's will and estate. So much to do," Dominic said between breaths.

"If you need me to do anything, let me know...I mean, I can take Raven for a few days, so you can concentrate on what you have to do," Poe offered, then regretted it instantly. Fear kicked in. What if she said something stupid in front of Raven? What if she couldn't handle Raven alone? What if she traumatized her any further?

He stared with huge, doe-like eyes. "You'd do that for me?"

"Yeah, I am her godmother, after all." *No take backs.*

"Thank you. I mean, she's napping now, but when she gets up, she wouldn't mind staying at her Great Aunt Lily's house." He smiled and relaxed his shoulders, then took a sip of his coffee.

They heard another knock on the door. After excusing himself, Dominic rose from his chair and walked to the door. From where she was seated, Poe heard voices. Who was there?

Dominic came back into the kitchen followed by Oliver and Kate. Kate looked like a pageant queen with her fake, plastic smile and perfect blonde hair. She was no Beyoncé or Mary J. Blige. Poe sighed. She didn't plan to disrespect Oliver's new woman despite all the rumors she had overheard. If Kate made him happy, then Poe had no right to say anything. She didn't want to make friends, but she could remain civil.

Poe extended her hand. "Hi. You must be Kate."

Kate shook her hand. "Hi."

"Oliver was right; you're very beautiful." Poe didn't think it would hurt to tell a little white lie—anything to help Oliver.

"Thank you." Kate grabbed Oliver's arm and rubbed her hand up and down it as if claiming her terrority. Poe looked away.

"Do you guys want coffee?" Dominic asked.

"Nah, that's okay," Oliver answered. Poe turned to face him, and he was already staring at her. Kate frowned. What was he thinking? Jenna had told her outlandish tales of how Kate would jump any female that may steal Oliver's attention from her. At times, Poe had laughed, figuring Jenna was exaggerating. But what if she wasn't?

Since Kate never bothered to respond, Poe asked, "Kate, how about you?" *Is she the type to let her man answer for her?*

Kate pouted. "I'm good."

"We actually came to visit you, Dominic." Oliver rubbed the back of his neck. "To see how you were doing, or to see if you needed anything."

"Great minds think alike." Dominic winked at Poe.

Kate stared at Oliver with both hands on her hips. "Did you know *she* would be here?"

"No." Poe noticed that for the first time, Oliver made eye contact with his girlfriend. What was it with men? Did they want to see a catfight? If so, she would gladly order one on pay-per-view as long as she didn't have to participate.

Dominic rolled his eyes. "It's not like the idea is so far-fetched. Of course, she came to visit me. That's what friends do." Everyone looked at him. "Do you have friends, Kate?"

"Yes, I—"

"Well then. You should understand the situation and give Oliver a break."

"I just meant there's a difference between a coincidence and an actual plan of meeting again. Who knows what they talked about on their ride *alone* from the airport."

Poe got up and stood beside Dominic, sipping her coffee. She felt it was necessary to have a bodyguard at the moment. Who knew if she could come out of this unscathed. It should have been a time for grieving, not defending herself against something she didn't do. "We talked about you. Oliver couldn't stop gushing about how wonderful you are and how much he loves you." Poe smiled, hoping Kate couldn't see through her lies. If she needed to stroke Kate's ego to gain peace, then Poe had no problems doing so.

After listening to a lengthy monologue of how Oliver and Kate were the perfect couple, everyone headed to the living room. Oliver squatted on the loveseat, and Kate sat on his lap. The rest seated themselves on the couch. No one spoke.

Poe observed the paintings and sketches on the wall; she smiled. She had drawn and colored everything, which Jenna had framed. She stood and walked over to the corner wall near the closet door. She stared at the haunted house near a graveyard on top of a scary hill. It was the first thing Poe had given Jenna in college. It amazed her that Jenna had kept it all those years.

Jenna had been obsessed with Edgar Allan Poe and Tim Burton. She loved the Gothic aesthetic. Poe figured that's why they got along so well in college. Jenna had loved Poe's name and even named her daughter after the famous poem.

"Thank you all for coming over. Sorry that I'm not better company," Dominic said, breaking the silence, which snapped Poe back to reality.

She turned to face everyone. "It's fine. I mean, if you were chipper or acted like everything was hunky-dorey, I'd have to give you the side eye."

Dominic and Oliver smiled.

"I don't think you should be so rude." Kate put her two cents in. Poe began to understand why Jenna had disliked her.

"It was a joke. *Hence,* all the smiles."

Kate folded her arms across her chest. "Well, I didn't find it funny."

Oliver sighed and slouched into his seat.

"Sorry for you. Giving someone the side eye is something Jenna and I used to say all the time."

Kate rolled her eyes.

A voice in the background said, "Daddy, Daddy." Dominic jumped up from the couch.

"I'll go with you." Poe needed to get away from Ms. Kate. First impressions meant everything to Poe, and Kate failed miserably.

"WHAT WERE YOU THINKING?" Oliver whispered after Poe and Dominic left.

Kate blushed. "She started it."

"She's been nothing but nice to you."

"No, she's been killing me with kindness." She pointed her finger in his face. "There's a difference, and if you didn't have her on a pedestal, you could tell the difference."

Oliver frowned. "Excuse me?"

"I see the way you keep staring at her. It's like I'm not even in the room."

Kate's jealousy was one of the reasons Oliver didn't love her. She could turn anything minor into a soap opera, but he hated drama—she seemed to live for it. He tapped Kate on the leg, signaling he wanted to get up. She hesitated. Worry crept on her face. She tried to pull him back by grabbing him by the hand. Avoiding her gaze, he shook his hand away and walked to the same spot where Poe had stood earlier. He admired the haunted house while collecting his thoughts.

Poor Dominic had to reel in Kate in the kitchen. Somehow, Kate always managed to make any situation about her. "I admit it's crazy having Poe here, but you shouldn't be disrespectful. She hasn't done anything to you."

Kate shifted in her seat and folded her arms across her chest. "That's rich; you're defending her. Really, Honey? She's so fake." She juggled her breasts. "Oh, let me be center of attention by standing while everyone sits, so they can admire my big, fake boobs and fat ass."

Oliver gave her a stern look. "Kate."

"You have to understand that this is hard for me. I'm here when I know Dominic could care less about me, and Jenna definitely hated me. Then, here comes Poe, who fits right in. People accept her with open arms and ignore me like I'm nothing."

Ignore? It's hard to ignore someone when they continue to make a fool of themselves. "Take a breath and calm down. I don't want you to feel uncomfortable. Please. Try for me, then I'll owe you big time."

She bit her bottom lip, twirling her hair around her finger. "You can repay me by bringing your fine ass over here."

"One second." Oliver admired the painting again.

"Are you kidding me? I'll throw that raggedy ass painting in the trash where it belongs. I'm not stupid; I know Poe created it. Probably why you're drooling."

"We came here to support Dominic. He doesn't need to hear any bullshit, and neither do I. Do you want me to take you home?"

"You'd like that, wouldn't you? To have Poe all to yourself without me ruining your moment," Kate said in a disgusted tone.

"I really don't get you right now." Or any of the other times she had acted jealous.

RAVEN, WITH TIRED EYES and hair disheveled, sat in the corner of her bed. Poe and Dominic sat down on the edge. "Daddy!" Raven gave him a hug.

"Sweetheart, want to stay with Poe for a couple of days?"

"Yes. Poe, I'm a big girl now."

"I see." Poe smiled. "Guess where we're staying?"

Raven looked hopeful. "Disneyworld?"

"Disneyworld? No, someplace cooler like your Aunt Lily's."

"Yea!" She clapped. "Is Daddy staying with us?"

"No," Dominic answered.

"Good, then girls' slumber party." Raven gave Poe two high-fives, as if they had joined a secret club.

"Help me pack," Dominic said.

"Okay, Daddy." She climbed down and grabbed her suitcase out of the closet.

Poe looked around the room, full of stuffed animals, a pink desk, dresser, bed sheets, and even pink wallpaper. Poe grabbed a photo from the nightstand and caressed it with her finger. It was Jenna, Dominic, and Raven standing on the pier as one happy family. Poe smiled and picked up the teddy bear next to her.

Poe wondered if Raven was a crier, someone who got homesick at the end of the night. The little girl had visited Poe quite often in Pittsburgh, but she was always with her parents. Poe had no idea how Raven would react being alone with her. She didn't even know if Dominic had explained that her mom was gone. What if Raven asked about death or Heaven? If so, should Poe discuss it with her?

Dominic carried the suitcase while Raven held Poe's hand. They walked into the living room.

"Hi, Ollie." Raven waved. "Hi, Kate." She wasn't as enthusiastic as before. Kate had a way of bringing everyone's spirits down. "I'm having a slumber party with Poe at Aunt Lily's."

"Oh yeah?" Oliver asked.

"Really, I'm not lying. I promise." She let go of Poe's hand, ran to Oliver, and snuggled up against him. He picked her up, so she could sit on his lap. Raven grabbed the TV remote and turned on cartoons. Poe could handle the Cartoon Network for a few days straight. She needed some comedy or silliness surrounding her, so she wouldn't break down and cry.

Oliver and Poe shared a look. He smiled. It seemed like he didn't hate her, and she knew she didn't despise him. She hoped he would help her baby-sit, depending on what Ms. Kate would allow. After all, he was the one who loved kids.

"Raven, are you ready to go?" Poe asked.

"Yeah." Raven wrestled out of Oliver's embrace.

He rose from the loveseat. "We can drive you."

Kate frowned and put her hands on her hips. Poe sighed. She really wasn't in the mood for round two.

Raven dashed to her dad and hugged him again. Dominic bent down to kiss her cheek. "Sweetheart, I love you."

"I love you too, Daddy." Raven glanced down at the floor, frowning. "I love Mommy too."

Poe glanced in Oliver's direction, then lowered her eyes to the ground. She and Kate stood up at the same time, wiping away tears that strolled down their cheeks.

"Oh man, I forgot my books. Poe, will you read me bedtime stories?"

"Sure."

Raven skipped to her room.

Chapter Four

Silence lingered in the car even though it was packed with four people. Poe and Raven sat in the back. From the corner of her eye, Poe noticed Oliver looking at her in the mirror. She busied herself, fidgeting with the suitcase that lay near her feet. Raven told her about her favorite cartoons. Poe pretended to listen.

She felt envy toward the little girl, who didn't feel the tension in the car. It must be nice to be full of innocence and naivety. To not understand the emotional toll it took being near an ex and his new girlfriend, especially when the new girlfriend wanted to flaunt it in her face. How did Poe get in this predicament anyway? The plan was to stay in a hotel. Why had she let Oliver talk her out of that so easily?

She shook her head and looked out the window. Was it a good idea to leave Dominic alone in the house all by himself? Maybe she should have offered to stay at his place to look after his daughter. That way he would have someone to talk to.

Even though her stomach cramped from not eating all day, Poe was not motivated to enjoy a meal. All she wanted to do was curl up in the fetal position and cry herself to sleep. She had sobbed last night, and then this morning in the shower, but she had plenty of tears left. Yet, she couldn't cry in the car—not in front of Oliver and Kate. And what about Raven?

Poe sighed and looked at the little girl. She needed to snap out of her funk if she wanted to baby-sit her properly. She tried to clear her mind and absorb Raven's descriptions of *Dora the Explorer, Spongebob Squarepants,* and *Care Bears.*

"Honey, you're dropping them off right? Then we can go to dinner," Kate said in an annoyed tone, as if she was tired of their company in the back seat.

"Who's them? My name—my name is Raven."

"Kate was using a pronoun," Poe said.

Raven placed her index finger on her lip. "Pronoun?"

Poe patted her shoulder. "Yes, I'll teach you all about it later if you want."

Kate must be ex-phobic; that could be the only explanation why she didn't speak civilly at Dominic's place, and now Kate was trying her best to get Oliver away from her.

"Honey?"

"Actually, I'm staying a little while. I want to see my mom." He tapped the steering wheel. "Then we can go out to eat."

Kate pouted, folding her arms across her chest. She stared out the window.

He sighed. "What's the problem? I said we'll go after I see my mom."

"I've been waiting since last night for our date. Can't you visit her tomorrow?"

"Please don't throw that back in my face. It's not like I stood you up on purpose." Oliver gripped the steering wheel. "How can you sit there and ask me not to visit my mom after you know what happened?"

"Please. Like you really want to see her. You just want to be up under your ex, and I'm not allowing it!"

"You're losing it, Kate. I'm not playing your game."

If this was a game, Poe could only imagine when Kate was really angry. Jenna hadn't been lying when she said Oliver had a handful. Raven perked up and stopped playing with her teddy bear. She must like witnessing drama as much as her mom did.

"If it makes you feel any better, Kate," Poe said. "I have a boyfriend back home."

"Like it matters."

Raven hugged her teddy bear. "Leo is nice. He buyed—he buyed me a slice of pizza once, and we played Mario Kart."

Like it matters. Kate must have heard the story of how Poe and Oliver ended up together. When they were twenty-two, Oliver was dating someone else, and Poe had just moved in with Jenna after college graduation. She met Oliver through Jenna. Poe liked men who looked into her eyes and studied her. Oliver was like that. Many times, Poe had caught him staring at her. Eventually, they had their first date at Four Leaf Clover. Oliver was Poe's first love, the one she lost her virginity to. The details were kind of blurry regarding whether or not he had broken up with the other girl first. They had followed their hearts. Poe could see why she'd be a girlfriend's enemy. That one incident would forever brand her as the 'relationship killer.'

Poe's first time was in the back of Oliver's Jetta; she observed the back seat and grinned. Reminiscing about that hot, passionate night made Poe forget her stomach cramps. She knew she shouldn't be thinking about Oliver. It was wrong, yet it felt as if it was meant to be. Memories of him were a part of her life.

FOR A SPLIT SECOND, Oliver peeked in the rearview mirror to look at his little cousin. He never knew Raven had met Leo; Jenna and Dominic had failed to mention that. Perhaps Leo and Poe were more romantically bonded than the impression he had. Images of his ex and her new man holding hands out in public rippled through his mind. He imagined them meeting with each others' families, as if they were in a serious relationship. Oliver gulped when he imagined Poe getting intimate with Leo. It had taken Poe a while to open up to him, to allow him to knock her wall down, so why did Leo get off easy? What was so special about him?

Oliver was tired of being the nice guy, the one who set his happiness aside for everyone else. Starting today, he would fight for what he wanted. The embrace at the airport and stolen glances of Poe wasn't enough for him. Oliver needed to be close to her again—emotionally and physically. His stomach clenched. Why couldn't Poe be his?

Oliver made a u-turn.

Raven gasped. "Ollie, this is the wrong way to Aunt Lily's house."

"I know. I have to make a pit stop first." Oliver focused on the road, avoiding Kate's icy glare. He stared at the taillights of the car in front of him. He swallowed a knot in his throat while looking the other way. He wanted to dodge the sidewalk at all costs. They passed the boutique where Jenna was killed. In his peripheral vision, he noticed the yellow caution tape and frowned. His heart sank.

Did Poe see the scene of Jenna's accident? What is she thinking about at this moment? She's so quiet. I wish I had a paid subscription to read her mind all day.

Oliver's destination was the Ruby Tuesdays's parking lot. Oliver parked the car and left the engine running. Everyone gave him a questioning look, yet Poe seemed the most curious. In the next minute, she would probably think he was an asshole, which he couldn't bear, but hopefully Poe would let him show her that he was still the guy she had fallen in love with.

He pulled out his wallet from his back pocket. "You want a restaurant so badly, here you go." He extended a hand filled with cash. "Here's money for dinner, a tip, and cab fare."

Kate's hand was gripped on her knee. "Honey—"

"Here. Take it and get out of my car." No more Mr. Nice Guy. No more Mr. Pushover.

"Honey—" Kate pouted, squeezing her eyes tightly. Fake crying wouldn't work this time. She had fooled him when they first began dating, but once she revealed her dream was to win an Oscar, Oliver wised up, which wasn't hard for him to do since Kate always went through the same routine before a tear fell from her eye.

"Take the money and get out. I want to grieve with people who cared about Jenna. I want to grieve with people who won't make today about themselves."

Like clockwork, tears fell down both sides of Kate's cheeks. "I'm sorry, Honey."

Oscar indeed. "It's too late for half apologies. Bye, Kate."

She caressed his cheek. "No, I'm not going anywhere."

"If someone tells you to do something, you should do it so you don't get a time out," Raven lectured.

Kate snatched the bills out of Oliver's hand, then got out of the passenger side, and slammed the door. He could see her in the rearview mirror as he drove off. Good thing she didn't have a key to his apartment. Otherwise, all his clothes would be drenched in bleach. She had the audacity to do that to her ex. What did he see in her again? Maybe deep down, he was punishing himself for not fighting for Poe to stay in Rhode Island.

Chapter Five

Oliver stood at the kitchen counter beside Poe, her soft hand grabbing for paper towels. If only she would glance her lovely brown eyes at him.

"Sweetie, get plates," Oliver's mom said.

Poe reached for plates; Oliver admired her figure while she stood on her tippy toes.

He was desperate for her attention—a glance, a smile, a frown, a headshake, anything—but she turned away from the counter. *Why is she avoiding eye contact?* He followed behind, pulling out a seat for her, but she walked around the table to sit on the other side.

Oliver sighed when his mom sat beside her; Raven joined him on the other side. A warm feeling had washed over him when his mother hugged Poe. He didn't think he'd see that again. He hadn't imagined Poe returning to Rhode Island. It was nice to see them both in the same room. It gave him hope that he and Poe could get back together. He had made progress at the airport and in the car ride; now, he shot it all to hell with his temper tantrum in the parking lot. He couldn't handle it if Poe looked down on him. He bet Leo wouldn't have done that.

Too late to take it back now.

Poe didn't like acting on impulse, and that's exactly what Oliver had done. One minute he was talking—no, screaming—at Kate, and another he practically—no, actually—threw her out of the car. He was better than that. That was no way to treat a woman.

Oliver frowned when Poe nibbled at the crust of her pizza. Poe loved pizza but had barely taken two bites. The silence in the kitchen tormented him. No one made eye contact or really took notice of anyone's presence. Even Raven stared off into la-la land.

"No boys allowed at the slumber party." Raven glanced at Oliver.

Karma?

He protested, "Can I at least stay for a minute to finish eating and talk to my mom?"

Raven hummed to herself, looked up at the ceiling, and pressed her index fingers to her lips.

"Wait. Why aren't boys allowed?" Poe asked.

"Because boys—boys have cooties."

Laughter echoed in the kitchen, and Oliver began to relax. Finally some socializing was going on. Now, everything seemed familiar. He didn't care if he was the butt of a joke as long as everyone cheered up.

Blushing, Poe glanced at Oliver, then turned to Raven. "Oliver should stay. I know a secret about him."

"Really?" Raven looked at her with delight.

"Yeah. He should stay because his best friend is Santa."

Raven looked at him like he was a celebrity. "WHAT!?"

"That's not all. The Easter Bunny and Tooth Fairy are his best friends too."

Raven slid out of her seat and gave Oliver a hug. The grease from her fingers stained his shirt, but he didn't care. "Ollie's allowed at the slumber party!"

"Thank you, Raven." Oliver grinned. Poe's lips curved into a smile. Did Poe feel the same way as him? The way he itched to close the gap between them? Why did she sit so far away?

Once Poe and Raven left the kitchen, Oliver and his mom cleaned up. He ran the water in the sink. "Mom, I got everything."

"Like hell you do." She stood behind him and patted him on the back. "I'm helping."

"Mom, are you okay?"

His mom stared blankly into space, her hands moving the dishtowel in a circular motion around the plate. Instead of putting each dish in its proper place, she stacked everything on top of the counter. "I will be...I hate that Jenna's gone, but I know Brady and Olivia were happy to be reunited with their daughter again." She wiped tears from her eyes. "People endure tragedies, but they move on. Their loved ones help with that." She kissed Oliver on the forehead. "How long is Poe staying?"

"I think all week."

"Will you fight for her or just let her go? I figure you came to your senses since you're here with her and not Kate. Where is Kate anyway?" She splashed soapy water in his direction. "Yes, I asked two questions, and I expect you to answer both."

Oliver stepped back. "I plan to fight. I can't lose her twice."

His mom's eyes beamed with pride. "That's what I want to hear."

"And about Kate...well she was tripping the second she heard what I did this afternoon. I was tired of her snide comments. Seriously, she couldn't just let me have this day. She had to make it all about her. It's not like it was six months later, and I was still grieving. It's only been a day—heck, not even twenty-four hours yet." Oliver rubbed the back of his neck; hot, soapy water ran down his skin, making the collar of his shirt wet. "Right before coming here, I dropped Kate off at Ruby Tuesday's. She's probably home by now."

His mom smiled like the cat from *Alice in Wonderland*. "Well, you know the rules if you decide to stay tonight—no hanky panky."

Oliver's neck flushed, and heat rose to his face. "Mom!"

POE DIDN'T KNOW IF a four-year old could wash themselves. Apparently not. Raven splashed in the bubbles like a mermaid. Her hair was soaking wet as she played with her rubber ducky. Poe took charge and wiped her with a soapy washcloth.

Her phone rang, and she rose to her feet. Wiping her hands on a towel, she grabbed it off the sink. She looked at the caller ID before answering. "Hey, Dominic. Are you okay?"

"Hey, Poe. I don't want to lie to you, so I'll say I've been better." He chuckled softly. "I'm actually tired, so I wanted to say good night to Raven before I head off to bed. Has she been good so far?"

"Yeah."

"That doesn't sound like Raven...hey, My Love's funeral is Wednesday at 11 AM. Since you're at Aunt Lily's, can you tell her too? And, I'll give Oliver a call."

"Actually, he's here too; I'll just tell them both." Poe wiped a tear from her eye, and took a deep breath. She had to get it together. She couldn't let Raven see her upset.

She walked slowly to the bathtub, almost tripping over a rug. Poe caught herself, happy her phone didn't get wet. She put it on speaker.

"Hey, Sweetheart, it's Daddy."

Raven waved. "Hi, Daddy."

"You being good for Poe?"

"Uh huh, I'm taking a bath, so we can have a slumber party. Ollie is invited too even though he's a boy. He is best friends with Santa, the Easter Bunny, and the Tooth Fairy."

Dominic talked to Raven a little while longer, then he directed his attention back to Poe. "Your night so far sounds juicy. I can only imagine what tomorrow will bring."

"I'm sure your little reporter will give you every detail." Poe laughed, splashing water on Raven. She soon regretted it, sure that Raven would think it was okay to splash back.

"Thanks for everything."

"No problem." She hung up the phone. Luckily, Raven was not in revenge mode; she was playing with bubbles. "I'll let you stay in there for a little while longer, then you'll get out." Poe logged onto the internet, looking for an affordable flight from Providence to Pittsburgh that would have her home Sunday. She couldn't find any later flights like she wanted. The only one available was a flight that left on Thursday at 6 PM. She bit her bottom lip, then reserved it.

Chapter Six

Poe and Raven changed into pajamas in the bathroom, then Raven skipped to the couch. It must be nice to be a Toys-R-Us kid; maybe that's why Poe was afraid to grow up. She walked into her room and didn't bother turning on the lights.

Poe had come for Jenna's funeral, but she was scared. It would be the first one she ever attended; usually if someone close to her died, she would find a reason to avoid the wake or funeral. She didn't want to see anyone in a casket. She didn't want to be packed in a church with a bunch of people crying, and she didn't want to see someone lowered into the ground. She feared she could never get that image out of her head. She wanted to remember her late friends and family members when they were alive and happy; they deserved to be thought of that way.

Poe fell back into her bed and planted both hands on her chest, like in movies when a character lay in a casket. She closed her eyes and held her breath for as long as she could. Poe gasped for air and thought that's how Jenna was in the funeral home, except Jenna was not experimenting.

Poe sighed. She didn't have time to think about herself. She had to consider Raven's feelings as well, and that little girl would be upset if she went out there and canceled the slumber party. "Get it together. You can do this," she whispered.

She entered the living room with a poker face. She had to seem okay—had to fake the funk—because it only took one person to ask her "what's wrong", then she couldn't stay strong.

Poe sat on the very end of the couch beside Raven, who was eating popcorn. Three DVDs were on top of the television set. There was a bowl of popcorn between Raven's legs, and chips and juice boxes on the coffee table. Oliver stood to turn the movie on; it was nice of them to wait for her.

They planned to watch three Disney movies—*The Lion King, Mulan,* and *The Little Mermaid.*

"Do you want popcorn?" Raven asked her.

Poe shook her head. She really didn't want to be the bearer of sad news, but she decided to get it over with. "Dominic just called. The funeral is Wednesday at 11 AM."

Please don't kill the messenger.

The remote dropped from Lily's hand as she covered her mouth. Oliver hung his head. Lily rose and kissed everyone on the cheek. "I'll see you guys tomorrow; I'm going to bed."

"Good night."

Poe hoped she was all right. Lily was just like her; they both hid their feelings behind sarcasm or the plain ole changing-the-subject tactic. Hopefully, she'd feel better in the morning. All she needed was alone time, exactly what Poe craved. She needed to let all her emotions out, but wouldn't dare do it in front of an audience. Poe would write in a diary before sharing her feelings, but if someone needed to vent, Poe was a great listener. In fact, she hoped Oliver would share his pain with her.

Instead of watching the next movie, Raven wanted to watch *The Lion King* again and again. She leaned into Poe's side, so Poe wrapped her arm around her. From the corner of her eye, Poe saw Oliver staring at her.

Hakuna Matata. After hearing the song three times, Poe started to believe in "no worries." It was a good movie but maybe not the best one since it dealt with death. They should have gone for *The Little Mermaid.*

She heard soft snoring. Raven had fallen asleep using Poe's breast as a pillow. "I'll put her to bed." Poe lowered her eyes to the floor. She had avoided going into Jenna's old room; now was the time to face the music.

"No, I'll do it," Oliver volunteered, as if he understood her dilemma.

Poe smiled weakly and watched him walk away with Raven in his arms. Why did he stay? Was Oliver avoiding his apartment? Maybe he would find Kate camped outside his door. Maybe he feared Poe would not do a good job taking care of his little cousin. Maybe Oliver blamed Poe for his outburst in the car, her presence bringing out all the bitter memories.

Bitter for him, perhaps. Poe cherished each and every moment with him. No. She shouldn't be thinking about that. She was certain he liked Kate. Granted, his girlfriend was a little mouthy, but that was understandable. She had been uncomfortable around her. Besides Kate and Oliver's back and forth seemed to be their routine as a couple.

Poe forced back tears; she had enough troubles and sorrows occupying her mind. She didn't need to think about Oliver. Not just yet.

She heard him walking out of the bedroom. Rubbing the back of his neck, he glanced at her. Hesitantly, she tugged a lock of hair behind her ear to avoid his gaze. She knew he was nervous. But why? Did she make him nervous? Maybe he wanted to let out his frustration? She took a deep breath, waiting for his sexy, deep voice to scold her, like he did Kate in the car. What was that anyway? Poe had never seen that side of Oliver before; she didn't even know he was capable of such aggressive behavior.

Slowly, Oliver made his way to the couch and sat down beside her, so close that their shoulders brushed. She swallowed hard. Surely, this wasn't the way to show one's frustration. When he didn't speak for a while, she focused her attention at the television screen rolling the end credits of the movie.

Say something. Anything. "Well, it's pretty late."

That nap on the plane was nothing; if allowed, Poe could've slept all day. Besides, it wasn't a good idea to spend so much alone time with Oliver. He made her feel like an insecure schoolgirl.

Oliver stood. "Can I see you tomorrow?"

She nodded. "If you want." Hopefully, he would make up with Kate by then, which would put him in a better mood.

She walked him to the front door, admiring the shirt that clung to his strong muscles. Why did he have to look so handsome? She tried to stop thinking of her ex in that way, but it was hard. Precisely why they shouldn't be alone. Poe didn't trust herself around him, and she didn't want to screw things up with Leo. Especially since he was her shoulder to cry on last night. That had meant a lot to her. He made her feel like she was the only woman in the world.

As Oliver put his hand on the knob, Poe turned around, heading towards the living room. The dim light from the television illuminated the room. Poe collected the bowl from the coffee table and put it in the kitchen sink. When she turned around, she bumped into a strong body, causing her to gasp.

"Sorry," Oliver said.

"You scared me." Poe took a step back to put some distance between them. She stared into his mesmerizing eyes, then quickly lowered her gaze.

"I just wanted to apologize for earlier." He readjusted his baseball cap, cheeks flushed red. "You or Raven shouldn't have had to see that. I think I was just tired. I'll talk to Kate, but I wanted to clear the air with you first. I hope you'll forgive me."

Why me? Oliver hadn't said anything to me. He should be apologizing to Kate. "I understand." Poe shrugged her shoulders because she didn't know what else to do.

He sighed, looking more relaxed, as he leaned into the counter and stared at her. A smile crept across his lips.

Why was Oliver studying her? Did she want him to leave? No. God help her, she wanted to stay up all night talking to him. About everything. About anything. Her throat dried. Poe felt guilty wanting him to stay. She thought she was over him, that he was history, but there had to be a reason why she had asked Leo not to join her.

"I'm happy you're here even though it could have been during better circumstances," Oliver said.

Poe fidgeted with her hands, holding back the look of pain that crept into her eyes. "Thank you for putting Raven to bed."

"Sure." He held her hands, keeping them still. She looked up and connected her gaze with his. She hated how good it felt, how calming it was. "I can't believe you're here. I can't believe we're talking." His eyes brightened in excitement. Or was it surprise?

Poe tried to hold back a smile but failed. "You said that already."

He let go and played with the cabinet handle like it was a new toy. "I know, I just never thought I'd see you in Rhode Island again. That's all."

Oliver's penetrating stare made the hairs rise on the back of her neck. A bead of sweat broke on her forehead. He wiped it away, and Poe tore her gaze from his as she lowered her eyes to the floor. She didn't deserve his attention. It'd be so much easier if Oliver hated her, if he had moved on with his new girlfriend.

The kitchen was quiet, heightening her anxiousness. "It's good seeing everyone again, especially your mom." Good. Keep the focus on his family, not him.

He smirked, mischief in his expression. "Everyone? Even me?"

Oh no, he was opening a whole can of worms. Keep it friendly. Don't flirt. Even though Poe wanted to express that she had missed him, she answered, "That's what *everyone* means."

Oliver moved closer. "Do you love him?"

She didn't know where to go. Leaning against the counter, Poe inhaled the scent of his cologne. A flash of him, his bare chest over her, danced through her mind. She shook her head, as if this would rid her of the memory. "No," she blurted without thinking. "Do you love Kate?" What was she doing?

He dipped his head down to hers and ran a fingertip just above her collarbone, which always sent a sensation of heat, a wanting need, rippling through her. He was the only one who knew exactly how to touch her...where to touch her...

"No," he whispered near her ear, his warm breath burning all hesitation and doubts, before he tipped his head just right, letting his bottom lip brush against her cheek.

She didn't shy away. She turned and aligned her face to his, and he gladly took the invitation and kissed her. A breath of longing escaped Poe's lips. With her hand pulling the back of his head, she deepened the kiss, leaning into Oliver, feeling him as he began to harden. He wrapped his arms around her, crushing her body into his. With a slight motion, he moved against her, harder now. Poe's heartbeat thrashed in her chest. She exhaled a humid breath against his neck, and pulled him by the hips, closer, rubbing him harder. Primal instincts took over. Without even knowing it, she let go of a low, delighted sound, soft, under her breath, before she entwined her hands around his neck and clutched Oliver even closer. With every passionate kiss, they couldn't keep their hands off each other, like they'd been stranded on a desert island.

Her nipples became harder against the brush of his fingertips, his slow-moving, wonderful thumb flicking it as it moved across, sending sensations she couldn't suppress.

"Wait. Oliver wait—I'm not staying," Poe said, coming up for air. He ignored her pleas and kissed her again. She gasped. How could she ever ignore his embrace? He dominated her with his lips and hands. Slowly, Poe moved her hands down his body to the front of his jeans, running daring fingertips across the large bulge, the tip pressed angrily at the confines of the fabric holding it in place, hard enough for her to feel it. "I hope you have a condom."

Poe's mind made her reasonable and careful while her heart throbbed for his touch. She was already hot and wet and ached for Oliver to be inside her.

He ran a hand down over her, feeling the dampness, feeling the heat. "Poe..."

He nuzzled her shoulder and tilted his head toward hers. Without any resistance, he tugged her shirt from her pants, and his fingertips traced imaginary circles across her upper abdomen, across skin smoother than silk. Moving higher, those same fingertips wandered over her bra, taking in the feel of lace and satiny fabric before running over the hard bead of her nipples.

His eyes were full of desire. He let go of her only to grab his wallet from his back pocket. Smiling seductively, Oliver took out a Trojan.

He pulled Poe into her bedroom, and shut the door behind them. Poe headed for the bed, but Oliver grabbed her arm. "The bed creaks." Guiding Poe up against the wall, he captured her lips again.

He slid his strong hands under her shirt, making his way up to her breasts. He massaged them, using his thumb; his touch was warm and teasing.

Oliver lifted her shirt to take it off, but she grabbed his hands, her breath quickened. "I want you inside me now."

He didn't need any more encouragement. He slowly peeled her panties down, spreading his fingers out as he ran the tips of them across both of her hips, moving in, then moving down her thighs, making sure to feel them both slightly quiver, his thumbs close, high, and in between.

"Oliver." She gasped. "Now! I need you now."

A finger separated her and ran the slickness over her most sensitive area. Her breath caught in her throat before a shallow sound moved through her open mouth. He circled that wonderful finger, sending waves of pleasure through her.

She sucked in a breath, deeply and sharply. "Please," she begged. "I can't wait any more."

"Not yet."

He circled again and again, feeling the slight gush of need, of pure excitement and anticipation. He dipped his finger in for some more, and she bucked in response. "Oliver."

She watched him bring his finger to his mouth, licking the juice from his fingertips. He unbuttoned his jeans. His erection pressed outward, still held back, still restrained by his briefs.

Just as she was about to reach out to touch him, he returned his hand to her. His sweeping fingertip had her breathing heavily, mouth open, her eyes clenched shut.

Quickly, he kicked off his pants. She took the opportunity to do the same. After putting the condom on, he lifted Poe by her butt like a caveman. The wall felt grainy, but as he entered her, she only focused on the sensations Oliver gave her, blocking out all the rest.

Oliver didn't have to worry if size or motion mattered because he was well endowed. With every slow, full thrust, he went deeper and deeper inside her. He raised her hips a little higher. She held him tighter, letting go of a tense, pleased breath, letting him know just how good it was. Her soft sounds only drove him further along, closer to wondrous release. His warm breath near her skin increased her yearning for him.

He kissed her neck and Poe knocked his hat off and pulled his hair. She was a loud moaner; it took all of her not to make an echoing sound. She put her mouth to his shoulder, biting him; he breathed harder on her neck. He moaned her name. Poe wanted to scream out, so she bit her own finger. She tasted blood in her mouth but didn't care.

Her muscles tightened, and the friction became too much. She pressed her knees together, and smashed them around him. Spasms quaked through her, and she clenched her mouth closed.

Still tightly embraced, she felt every throb as it slowed and calmed inside her, his release just seconds before hers.

POE TREMBLED UNDER the covers. Why couldn't Lily turn the air conditioner off during the night? She lay next to Oliver, both on their backs with their faces turned to each other. "The bed creaks, huh? And you know this how?"

"After prom, I brought my date over, and we fooled around. Good thing mom wasn't home."

"No hanky panky." She giggled. "I wonder if Lily would spank us if she found out."

"Nah, that wouldn't be punishment for you. You'd like it too much." Oliver moved closer to Poe. Him teasing her was a big deal because he was usually such a serious guy. She felt good seeing him comfortable around her again. Hopefully, no more silent treatment.

"You know today I couldn't help but remember when we did it in the backseat of your Jetta. You were my first," she whispered and kissed his hand.

Oliver closed his eyes, like he was trying to bring that moment to life. He kissed Poe on the shoulder blade. If he was ready for round two, she could handle it; she had to get warm somehow. "You were my first, too, in a way. I mean, I lost my virginity in high school, and I thought I loved my girlfriend at the time, but I didn't. You were the first girl I was *in love* with before doing it." He kissed her shoulder blade again.

Poe held her breath; he said all the right things that she didn't deserve. What had they done? What a way to repay Leo for his kindness last night. He would never look at her the same way, and she couldn't blame him. No wonder Kate disliked her. She was so 'the girl' who stole boyfriends. She fell in that position when she first met Oliver, and she just did it again.

Why does he have such a hold on me?

Chapter Seven

It wasn't Oliver's snoring that kept Poe awake. She didn't know why she couldn't sleep. Was it the realization she had slept with someone else's boyfriend? Or the fact that she had become disloyal to Leo? Shaking her head, Poe decided to try and get some work done. She got out of bed, removed her briefcase from the closet, and opened the bedroom door. Poe was surprised it wasn't locked. Good thing no one had walked in on them.

In the dark hallway, Poe walked into a stand, hitting her stomach. She covered her mouth with her hands, so she wouldn't scream, then felt her way along the wall to the bathroom.

Poe closed the door and turned the lights on.

She couldn't bring herself to open the briefcase on her lap. Poe rubbed her arms rapidly, trying to get warm. Why hadn't she brought a sweater? Within minutes, Poe lost all motivation to draw. Her stomach growled and cramped up. She held it and rocked back and forth; this gave her some relief, but she cried anyway. She didn't want Jenna to think she was a cold-blooded bitch for bringing her work with her. She knew Jenna was dead, but she believed in her heart that Jenna watched down on all of them, at least until she would be buried.

Poe thought about George from *Grey's Anatomy* when he was run over by a bus, how no one could identify him except for a mark on his hand. Had that been the same for Jenna?

It hurt to think that her best friend had suffered so much pain before dying alone. That there would probably be a closed casket. Happy memories of Jenna started to fade from Poe's mind. She didn't want that to happen. Poe sobbed so much that she got a headache, her head on top of her briefcase; she almost suffocated. She inhaled against leather until it felt like she would pass out from lack of oxygen, then she moved her head to the side and stared into space, breathing in cold air.

Suddenly, she sat up straight, and felt a sense of awareness. She whispered, "It's okay, Poe. You can do this." She released the latches on her briefcase, and took out her sketchpad, lead pencil, and black felt pen. The pages seemed to shriek, and her hand, as if in rebellion, shook so much that she couldn't draw a straight line. "Come on, Poe. Get it together." She attempted to draw again, her hand steady this time.

Poe's comic was about a group of friends, who were twenty-two, just graduated from college and trying to make it in the real world. Poe created two pages of her comic book in two hours. Now, her butt and legs went numb.

OLIVER WOKE UP TO AN empty bed. He felt on the nightstand for his cell phone and turned it on. It was 5:50 AM. Where was Poe?

He saw light through the crack under the bathroom door, so he knocked.

"Come in."

Oliver opened the door and saw Poe gathering papers that were spread all over the bathtub and sink. Not even looking up, she said, "Sorry. You need to use the bathroom?"

"What are you doing?"

She looked up. "I couldn't sleep." Her eyes were puffy, and her nose was red.

Oliver felt like someone had stabbed him in the heart. He sat on the edge of the tub, facing her; he leaned over, yearning to be closer. "What's wrong?"

She lowered her gaze to the floor. "Nothing. I just wanted to work on my comic."

"In the bathroom?" Of all the places in the house, why there? Did she want to avoid him at all costs that she would hide on the toilet instead of lay next to him in bed?

Poe gave a weak smile. "Why not?"

"How long you been up?"

"I don't know." Poe shrugged her shoulders and tucked a strand of hair behind her ear.

"I'm sorry. If I had known, I would've kept you company. I hope you know that you can wake me for anything."

Poe played with Oliver's hair. "That's okay; you don't have to keep me company. Go back to bed."

"I'm not leaving you in the bathroom." Maybe she didn't trust him enough to let her wall down. He wanted Poe to rely on him.

Poe sighed, frowning.

Did he repulse her this badly? "Poe?"

"What is so wrong with this room? I'm not a weirdo for being in here. Heaven forbid, I came up with the logic that it's the only room with a door, so I can keep the light trapped in. Good golly Miss Molly, I didn't want to work in the kitchen or living room because I had the logic and courtesy not to want to wake anyone up." Poe gathered the rest of her papers, and put everything in her briefcase, then slammed it down on the floor. "What is *so wrong* with the bathroom, Oliver?"

"You're not a weirdo." He could never believe the stories of how Poe had been a misfit in high school, how her classmates had laughed at her shyness and called her ugly. They must have been blind. She was perfect in Oliver's eyes—his version of Drew Sidora, except Poe rocked a brown sleek bob with red highlights.

Her eyes widened, as if Oliver had betrayed her by mentioning *weirdo*. Her classmates used to chant that when she walked down the hall. No wonder she hardly let anyone in; no wonder she pushed people away. Poe attempted to stand, and almost fell into the sink until she reached out and caught herself.

Oliver rushed to her side. "Are you okay?" He grabbed her arm, but she pushed his hand away.

"I'm fine. My legs are numb; it's not the end of the world."

"You're mad at me? You're mad at me because I'm trying to help you?" His voice cracked.

"I didn't ask for your help. Please leave me alone. Leave me alone *in this bathroom*."

Oliver didn't budge. He couldn't leave her alone; that was the whole point. It hurt him to know that Poe would rather fight than tell him what was bothering her. If Poe would talk to him, Oliver could fix it. "Poe, stop pushing me away. Talk to me." Oliver turned Poe around, so she could face him.

She shook her head, then her shoulders collapsed. She gazed at him with her beautiful brown eyes. "I'm sorry. I shouldn't have snapped at you. It's just...I'm so tired. I'm so tired and worn down, but I can't sleep. I can't sleep, so I thought I should do something productive, but I wish I was asleep instead...I'm sorry; I'm just tired." Poe's body shook. Tears rolled down her cheeks.

Oliver wrapped his arms around her. She squeezed him tightly. He wished he could take her pain away.

POE DOVE UNDER THE covers while Oliver laid her briefcase on top of her legs. He slowly walked to the other side of the bed, examining her. She blushed. She didn't mean for him to witness her outburst like that.

"You can finish drawing in here," he offered. His knight-in-shining-armor routine made Poe feel even more guilty. Having sex with Oliver shouldn't have happened. Why was he acting like everything was normal? Why didn't he feel regretful too?

Please don't make me face these feelings alone.

"I'm done," she said.

"Are you sure?"

"Yeah, thanks. I'll try to sleep now." She set the briefcase on the floor. "Can you turn off the lights?"

Oliver made his way across the room without hesitation. Instead of walking back to his side of the bed, he walked over to Poe and kissed her forehead. He crawled over her and lay on top of the cover, halfway leaning over her. With his head only two inches from hers, she couldn't turn to face him. "Are you sure you're okay?" he asked.

Poe gulped. "Yeah."

Oliver gently rubbed her back for a few minutes, then he began snoring. She closed her eyes tightly. She didn't want to see the dark shadows decorating the walls. It reminded her that she was facing her demons and weaknesses alone.

Chapter Eight

Poe was tired, yet she couldn't sleep, and it was far too late to keep trying once she heard the pitter-patter of feet running into her bedroom. She closed her eyes.

Raven stood on Poe's side of the bed. "Good morning."

Oliver grunted. "Good morning."

"Poe never read—never read me a bedtime story last night. Can she do it now?" Raven shook Poe by the shoulders. "Poe, wake up."

Poe didn't budge. As a prank, she planned to jump up and scare Raven when she least expected it.

"Actually Raven, I'll read it to you," Oliver said.

"No, I want—I want Poe to do it. Poe, wake up."

"Come on, Raven," Oliver said. "Let her sleep; let's go watch cartoons."

"NO!"

Poe couldn't pretend to be asleep any longer. If she did, this little diva may have Oliver tied up in a corner. She stretched and yawned; her prank would have to wait another day. Poe helped Raven climb over her, so she could squeeze in between them in bed. Raven snuggled up against the silky, satin purple pillows. She handed Poe a book.

This wasn't Poe's ideal way of spending her morning, but she didn't mind. "Sorry, I didn't get to read to you last night," Poe said.

Raven smiled. "It's okay—it's okay because you're reading it now."

Poe peeked over at Oliver, who was staring at the book's front cover. He looked hot for just waking up. Maybe last night was only meant to be a one-night stand, but it didn't mean she couldn't still admire him. Or maybe she was self-doubting like usual. All she knew for sure was that she shouldn't have yelled at him last night. He didn't deserve that.

Poe read the book on farm animals while Raven looked at each page intently. She tried her best to fake enthusiasm, but she couldn't get rid of the coarse tiredness in her voice. Raven put her hand on Poe's arm, then on top of the page. "You have to give each character a different voice. That's how—that's how Daddy and Mommy read it to me."

Of course it was. Poe sighed and started over. There was no point arguing with the little diva because it wouldn't solve anything. Eventually, Poe finished the twelve-page book.

"Now, we can watch cartoons," Raven said to Oliver.

"Okay."

Raven climbed over Poe with some help and ran out the door, forgetting her teddy bear and book. It was nice of Oliver to help her, even though it wasn't his responsibility. She wasn't going to object to getting more sleep since she hadn't slept last night. She had listened to Oliver's quiet snoring and breathing, as though it was a classical music CD.

Oliver gathered Raven's belongings and walked around to Poe's side of the bed. He leaned down and planted a kiss on her forehead.

"Thank you," she said.

"You know I'd do anything for you." He kissed Poe on the forehead again. How was she supposed to compose herself if he kept doing things like this? Did she even want to compose herself?

Oliver stood up to walk away, but Poe grabbed his hand. He caressed it and smiled.

"Let Raven know who's boss, and don't forget to use your best friends as an advantage," she teased. She enjoyed hearing Oliver's laughter. Now, that was something she could be used to waking up to.

OLIVER SLOUCHED ON the couch while Raven sat next to him. They watched the Cartoon Network; his little cousin talked his ear off about her favorite toys that she wished she had brought with her. She spoke of her barbies, doll babies, and stuffed animals. Raven described her best friends in great detail, so he paid attention in case she'd quiz him later. Raven made a habit of testing people, like a skilled analyzer. The last thing Oliver wanted to do was hurt her feelings by not paying attention.

He felt bad that Raven lost her mom because he knew the feeling of losing someone dear. His dad had left him at an early age. They hadn't spoken since. Not by Oliver's choice. He had no idea if his dad had started a whole new family, if he had any half-siblings out there. He didn't even know if his dad ever loved him, but since he'd never bothered to track Oliver down, Oliver assumed he didn't love him. What was wrong with him that made his dad stop loving him?

Oliver's dad had grown up in Providence. He had no idea where to start looking, and his dad had such an ordinary name. Oliver would probably have to search over one-hundred-thousand people and still wouldn't get a lead.

Oliver never told his mom about his interest in searching for his dad. He didn't want to hurt her. He didn't want her to think she wasn't good enough for him, but tragedies like his cousin's death motivated him to start investigating. He wanted answers before it would be too late.

For now, he was content to hang out with Raven and watch *Scooby Doo*. Anything was better than watching the Disney movie from last night.

"Ollie, can we watch *The Lion King*?"

Oliver smirked. He'd jinxed himself. After he turned on the DVD player, he sat back on the couch; Raven snuggled up to his side, so he put his arm around her. He hoped Poe was getting rest. Her freak-out in the bathroom had spooked him. Maybe the more she slept, the better she'd feel. He was happy that Poe seemed to be in a better mood this morning. Even though she wasn't an early riser, Poe hadn't kicked anyone out of the room. That was always a plus.

He had enjoyed watching Poe interact with Raven. They seemed like the perfect family. Hopefully, one day he'd have an official family with Poe.

"This is Poe's favorite movie," Raven said.

"I know."

"We watched—we watched it at her house every time we visited. *The Lion King* is Mommy's—Mommy's favorite movie too. Did you know that?"

"No, I didn't." Oliver would pay attention this time, knowing how much the Disney film meant to his little cousin. Perhaps this was her way of staying connected with her mom. He liked to think that Jenna—well, her ghost—was somewhere in this room watching the movie with them. Since Raven was a kid, did her innocence allow her to see ghosts? Could she see Jenna?

"Mommy, Daddy, and Poe are bestest friends. Did you know that?"

"Yes, I did." Sometimes Oliver was jealous that Jenna and Dominic met Poe before he did. He wished he would've visited Jenna on Morgantown's campus, but eventually he met Poe, and that was all that mattered.

"Who's your bestest friend?"

He tapped his foot along the floor. "That's a good question." Oliver had friends, but no one he'd call a best friend. His childhood buddy had went off to the army after high school, and died during battle. Oliver never quite got over that. Some days he wished he had been there with James. Instead, he got to see James's dad quite often at work.

Even though he was a townie, Oliver never really kept in touch with people he went to school with. He hung out with his family and co-workers. He didn't need many people in his life to be happy—Oliver needed only the ones he cared about and who cared about him.

Oliver tickled Raven's stomach. "You know who they are," he teased.

She laughed and squealed, looking at him like he was a magician, who could make Santa appear in the living room. "YES!" Raven laughed so hard she passed gas. It wasn't a silent one; her cheeks turned red. She raised her shirt over her mouth and nose. "Excuse me," she whispered.

It didn't stink, so Oliver didn't know why Raven covered her nose. She didn't act like her mom on everything. If Jenna would've farted, she would have laughed and went on about her business. She had been lactose intolerant, so she made a habit of passing gas back-to-back after eating certain foods. When they were pre-teens, Oliver and Jenna would play a game of how fast she could clear a room. She wasn't the dainty type at all. She never cared who was in the room. Oliver usually won with his guess of three minutes.

After college, Dominic moved into Oliver's apartment, and every morning they joked about Dominic's habit of keeping a bottle of air freshener by the alarm clock. Jenna would smile and eat her breakfast, usually clearing the room by her last bite.

It was funny the things people remembered about the deceased.

"Ollie, are you laughing at me?"

"No. Everyone farts. It's no big deal."

"It's your—your fault." She folded her arms across her chest. "You tickled me too hard."

Oliver was in a silly mood, so he tickled her again. "Like this." He laughed, and Raven giggled even harder and tried to wiggle out of his grasp.

POE LAY THERE LISTENING to Oliver and Raven enjoying each other's company. He would make a great father someday. She had heard through the grapevine that Kate wanted to start a family with him. Hopefully, she didn't mess that up for him. He deserved happiness.

She would just have to get over herself this week and keep him on track with his future goals. He shouldn't backtrack because she was in town. If she could help Oliver get back together with Kate or at least find someone suitable for him, then he couldn't confuse her. Yes, that's exactly what she would do today to make up for their mistake last night. It couldn't happen again, no matter how much either of them wanted it. They weren't kids anymore—it was time to grow up.

Poe figured if she had coffee, then she could concentrate on drawing again or baby-sitting Raven. Before she lifted the covers, her cell phone rang. "Hello?"

"Hey, Babe, you didn't call yesterday to let me know your flight went okay, so I'm calling now to check up on you," Leo said.

"This early in the morning?"

"It's not that early."

"Well, I haven't really talked to anyone since I landed. I texted Keisha; I guess I should've texted you and Mom and Dad too. Sorry." She should have also kept her lips to herself and stayed away from Oliver. Trust that she had more to apologize for.

"It's all right. I know you have a lot on your mind. That's why I wish I was there with you. So...what hotel you staying at?"

Good question. It should've been The Holiday Inn, but she allowed her ex to talk her into staying at his mom's house. She hesitated. "Ms. MacNamara."

"Is that a bed and breakfast?"

"No." Poe swallowed. "I'm staying with Jenna's aunt. Remember the place I lived in when I first moved to Rhode Island? Well, I'm here, even staying in my old room."

"Oh, well, that's good. You're not alone then." Leo didn't have a hint of curiosity in his tone, which Poe was grateful for. Now would not be a good time to discuss her indiscretion.

"No. In fact, I'm looking after Raven for a few days."

"Really? You alone with her; I can't picture it."

She snarled. "What? It's not like I'm the wicked witch of the east, or that I'm Ursula or any other storybook villain. We're doing just fine." It was better to start a fight than have to tell him Oliver was helping her baby-sit. It was the only way to get Leo to change the subject.

"Babe—"

"You know what, since I'm up now, I'm getting ready, so Raven and I can hang out. She remembered you by the way." She placed a fist on her hip. "She said you're really nice for buying her a slice of pizza and playing Mario Kart with her."

"She remembers that?" Leo asked in disbelief.

"Yes. It's not like she's a baby. She's pretty smart for her age."

"Babe, come on. You can't be mad at me for being shocked that you're with a kid. You're not exactly the motherly type, which is why I love you. We're both on the same page about not wanting children. I wasn't trying to be disrespectful. I promise. You can't tell me that you wouldn't be shocked if I told you that I was watching my nephews by myself. Let's face it, I'm not exactly the fatherly type either. Please don't be mad at me."

Leo's confirmation made her feel even less confident that she could handle Raven alone. Instead of getting Oliver's help, she'd need someone else. And, she knew she shouldn't be starting an argument with Leo, but his voice gutted her.

How could she cheat on him? They had only been dating for six months, but she shouldn't do anything that she expected him not to do.

"Leo, I got to go."

"You know what, I hurt you accidentally, but you're hurting me on purpose. You don't have to act like a bitch."

"Don't want me to be bitchy, don't want me to be grumpy, don't want me to have an attitude? Then, don't wake me knowing I'm not a morning person." Poe hung up the phone. Before she could set it down, it rang again. "Hello," she said, killing with kindness.

"You hung up on me!"

"Well, you're not listening. I've told you a billion times that I'm trying to get ready. I have plans with Raven; this meanie has plans with her goddaughter."

"Like what?" His tone was making her feel less guilty.

"What is this? Thirty questions? Okay, I want to take her to the pier, out shopping. We'll eat lunch and dinner. Have another slumber party."

"Well, I wouldn't want to bother you with your *busy schedule* and all. Maybe you can find the time to fit me in and call me later. Bye, Babe," Leo said sarcastically, then hung up.

Poe shook her head. Could she do anything right this week? She lay back down and closed her eyes.

OLIVER DECIDED TO MAKE breakfast. Raven sat on the counter beside the stove, and Oliver prayed she wouldn't accidentally burn herself. Dominic would never forgive him.

She was his little helper, so she handed him whatever he asked. Spread out on the counter, there were raw eggs in a bowl to make omelets, and in another bowl was pancake batter, and sliced peppers and onions. Every once in a while, Raven pretended to dip her hand in the bowl of eggs, like it was a game. Whenever Oliver would tell her to stop, she would squeal with laughter.

"Ollie, you stole Poe from me last night."

"What?"

"You heard me, Ollie. It was—was our slumber party, and Poe—Poe was supposed to sleep with me in my room. Not yours."

"I'm sorry. Do you forgive me?" Oliver grew up surrounded by female relatives at a young age; he realized it was best to apologize right away, whether the female was right or wrong. Fewer headaches.

Raven hit both index fingers against her lips while she stared at the ceiling. Oliver smiled. "Yes—Yes, I forgive you. Do you love Poe?"

"Yes, I do." Wasn't she a little too young to know what love meant?

"I thought so. You look at her the same—the same way Daddy looks at Mommy. Did you two jump on the bed last night?"

"Jump on the bed? No, we didn't."

Months ago, Jenna and Dominic had shared a story with him. Raven had walked in on them making love under the covers one morning. She snuck up on them and climbed on the bed. They had to compose themselves and come up with a story that they had been playing a game of jumping on the bed.

"Good. You two didn't play—play games, so she'll want to stay with me. I'll jump on the bed with Poe."

Only if Poe wants to go to prison. Oliver laughed, and Raven punched him on the shoulder. He rubbed the sore area. For a four-year old, she had a hard punch. "Don't laugh, and don't—don't try to steal my game."

"I won't. I promise." Oliver flipped pancakes and bacon. The food smelled so good that he was tempted to eat out of the skillet. Grease popped from the bacon, so Oliver lifted Raven off the counter.

They came to an agreement that they would tell everyone she had cooked breakfast. Apparently, this would make things right for stealing Poe the night before. Raven smiled and sang, "Poe and Aunt Lily will be so proud of me."

It was time to wake everyone up, so they agreed that Raven would get Poe, and he would get his mom. Oliver knocked and entered his mom's bedroom. She was lying in bed, watching TV. "Good morning, Mom."

She had bags under her eyes, like she hadn't slept. She was sitting up in bed, still under the covers. "Good morning. Did you stay last night?"

"Yeah."

"Good." She grinned, rubbing her eyes. "Is everyone awake?"

He noticed his mom didn't ask where he slept. Hopefully, she was on the same page, rooting for him and Poe to get back together. Poe would listen to his mom's advice. Oliver could have Raven and his mom in a cheering section with signs painted, 'Poe + Oliver'. Who says only sport teams need support and encouragement.

"I don't know. Raven is getting Poe now. Breakfast is ready." Hopefully, his mom wouldn't refuse to come down. If she did, he would fix her a plate and bring it up to her.

Oliver's mom turned off the television set and got out of bed. She threw on a thick red robe over her pajamas. While they went down the stairs, Oliver caught his mom's attention. "Play along that Raven cooked everything by herself." His mom grinned.

RAVEN SHOOK POE'S SHOULDER. "Poe, wake up," she yelled.

Poe sat up, jerking, almost knocking Raven down. She looked at Raven. "What's wrong?"

"Nothing, silly. Breakfast's ready."

"You go ahead." She head-butted her pillow twice. "I'll be out."

"No, we have to go together. We can't let the food—food get cold that I made."

Poe closed her eyes, yawning. "What did you make?"

"Everything." Raven's eyes beamed with pride.

Poe thought of all the possible injuries Raven could have encountered by being near the stove. On her watch, Raven could have been covered with third degree burns on her hands, or broken a leg or arm, or started a fire with a dish-cloth on top of the burner. It's not like Poe could say it was Oliver's fault.

Raven must be fibbing unless the breakfast was bowls of cereal. Warm cereal or warm milk didn't motivate Poe to want to eat. Poe sighed. Raven didn't mean any harm, but due to her own grumpiness, Poe found her to be a pest. "Fine. Let's go." She threw the covers off and slowly got out of bed. She grabbed her sweater off the chair and went into the kitchen with Raven.

Chapter Nine

In the middle of the table were full plates of light and fluffy pancakes, crispy bacon, omelets with green and red peppers, golden brown biscuits, and colorful fruit salad. *If Raven created all this, then I'm a rocket scientist.*

Raven sat at the end of the table, like she was the Queen of England. Poe sat on the right side of her, and Oliver sat on the left. Lily sat down beside him. Of course, he *had* to sit right across from Poe. She would have to avoid eye contact, so she wouldn't get lost in his deep, blue eyes.

Even though Poe had hunger pangs, she still wasn't motivated to eat. "Thank you," she said, directing it to the adults. Someone had placed a cup of coffee in front of her plate of an omelet and a pancake.

Lily smiled. "You're welcome. I know you're not fully awake until you get caffeine."

Poe had a hard time swallowing after chewing. It felt like the food was poison; that she might have to throw it up later. While she ate, the little diva stared at her. Why was Raven being so quiet? Why wasn't she eating? "We can't let the food get cold, remember?" Poe told her.

Raven pointed to her pancakes, but Poe didn't know what that meant. Lily rose from her seat. "Oh, she needs someone to cut her pancakes. Why didn't you say so, sweetie?"

"No, I'll do it." Poe grabbed her fork and cut. Lily sat back down.

"What happened to your finger?" Raven asked.

Huh? Poe glanced down at her hand; there was a dark, deep set of teeth marks on her right index finger. She had two options—lie or tell the truth. Lying would be the best option in this situation.

When Poe and her siblings were younger, her brother, Derek, spooked her constantly. He would tell her that the boogeyman hid in her closet and under her bed. Her parents never understood why she was so scared at night. Poe would scream in the middle of the night for someone to come check her room. Her parents were not pleased. Some nights, Keisha would sleep in bed with her.

Once, Derek had told Poe she would become possessed if she didn't hand over her desserts to him at the dinner table. Her parents thought she was so kind for giving Derek the dessert off her plate. If they only knew.

Her brother had also told her that whenever she'd get a scratch, during the healing process, ants could get in her body and suck all her blood. Her parents never understood why she trembled when the band-aid had to come off. To this day, Poe was still afraid of ants.

She considered telling Raven that she saw the boogeyman last night, and she'd been so scared that she bit her finger, but Poe figured that would not go over well. "I accidentally closed my hand in the closet door, so it made a bruise."

"A boo-boo," Raven corrected.

"Yes, it made a boo-boo."

"If you—if you kiss it, it'll feel better."

Poe immediately kissed her boo-boo, causing Raven to grin. "It's working already." She smiled.

She shared a look with Oliver. She couldn't help herself. He touched his shoulder, eyeing her with desire. These next few days would be hard to stay out of trouble. She couldn't believe she bit herself that hard. It all came back to her—the pleasure, the pain, the taste of blood. Then, she remembered how she'd walked into a stand, probably had a bruise on her stomach as well. Maybe she would get Oliver to kiss that boo-boo later.

No, I shouldn't think like that. Snapping out of an Oliver trance, Poe looked down at her half-eaten food. No more glancing across the table. *Keep the focus on Raven and Lily.*

While they ate, Raven studied everyone. "Um, this is so delicious. Mmmhmm. This—this is so delicious."

"Yes, Raven it is." Lily gave a thumbs up. "You cooked everything perfectly."

Raven laughed and clapped her hands.

Oliver laughed too. "It's really good."

Raven clapped again. Poe felt like everyone except her was in on a joke. Everyone kept staring at her. Was there a booger hanging from her nose? Did she have syrup around her mouth? Sometimes she was a messy eater.

Someone kicked Poe's leg hard. She yelped, then looked at Oliver, who was drinking his orange juice. She turned to Lily, who mouthed, "Tell Raven the food is good."

Poe rubbed her leg. No need for violence. "You want to know how delicious this food is?" She looked at Raven with a sly grin.

"How much?" Raven was wide-eyed, like a kid walking into Willy Wonka's Chocolate Factory.

"This food is so delicious that I've hardly touched my coffee. I never eat breakfast, Raven, and you managed to make me scarf down my food, my very delicious food."

Raven clapped and chuckled. For the rest of the meal, she talked everyone's ears off.

WHY DO I ALWAYS PUT myself in awkward situations? Instead of joining Raven in the living room, Poe decided to help Oliver clean up the kitchen. She couldn't say no.

"Do you work today?" Poe asked Oliver hesitantly.

"Not until Thursday." He raised an eyebrow, smirking. "I'm all yours until then. Is that all right?"

Poe blushed. Thursday. It dawned on her that she was leaving that day.

Before she could tell him the news, Raven walked into the kitchen. "Can I have a glass of milk?"

Poe gave a sly grin. "Can you just stay thirsty?"

Raven shook her head. "No, I need milk. Please, Poe."

Poe laughed, dropping her dishcloth. She walked to the cabinet, picked up a cup, and poured Raven some milk. Raven reached for it, but Poe waved her finger from side to side, and raised the cup high in the air. The little diva pouted. Poe giggled, then handed her the cup. Now, she understood why her older brother always picked on her. It was fun, but Poe knew not to let the teasing go on for too long. She wished someone had given Derek that memo.

I'm all yours until then. Is that all right? Raven had perfect timing because Poe wasn't sure how to answer her ex. She'd wanted to say in her most seductive tone, "Of course you can." In Poe's heart, she yearned to spend as much time with Oliver as possible, but her head was saying something completely different. She shouldn't mess things up for Oliver if she wasn't planning to stay in Rhode Island. Why start something she couldn't finish?

Raven finished her milk and left the cup on the counter. *Great, another dish.*

Poe picked up her dishcloth and peeked at Oliver. He was staring at her, as if he were waiting for her response. She knew what to do—go the friendly route. "Actually, you should go to the flower shop and pick up some roses for Kate. All women love roses."

"You don't like roses." Oliver's eyes, full of passion and lust, scanned Poe's body up and down, admiring her curves.

She glanced away, swallowing hard. "Point taken, but Kate probably does. I'm sure if you apologize for everything, roses would do the trick."

Preferably leaving out the part about last night—at least until she left. Poe wasn't much of a fighter. She didn't really want to test her boxing skills during the next couple of days. But if Poe got her butt kicked, she'd deserve it. Oliver used to be hers, but they were exes for a reason.

"You're silly." He laughed and handed her a dish with wet, soapy hands. He held onto Poe's hand for a second too long, but she avoided his eye contact. She forced down a pleasurable gasp that threatened to escape her lips.

"I've heard that once or twice." Plan A, getting Kate and Oliver back together had failed miserably. He wouldn't even entertain the thought. It made Poe wonder why he had spent eight months with Kate if he could let her go that easily.

Time for Plan B, pointing out someone new for Oliver. "How's Melinda?"

He shrugged his shoulders. "Fine. I guess."

"I wonder if she still likes you."

"You used to always say that when we were together. Melinda doesn't like me. Why do you think that?"

"A woman just knows. I mean, the way she couldn't take her eyes off you. The way she would stare when she thought no one was looking. Whenever me and Jenna hung out with her, Melinda would always bring you up. Come on, you know she has feelings for you. She's just too shy to say anything."

Oliver scooted his body closer to Poe's. "You're shy, but you let me know how you felt."

She laughed nervously as Plan B was circling down the drain fast. How could she do the honorable thing if he wouldn't let her? If she couldn't have him, she wanted Oliver with someone who could make him happy. Someone who could give him what he needed—a family. Poe knew Melinda wanted to be a mother someday.

"Let me see your finger," Oliver said. Poe hesitantly raised it, so he could see the bite marks. He leaned over and kissed it. "Feel better?"

She bit her bottom lip. "Yes." She threw the dishtowel down on the counter. She moved closer and stood on her tippy toes, their bodies touching. She regretted it, but it was too late. She lifted his shirt sleeve from his shoulder and gently touched his bite mark. She flushed when she remembered it. "Just like I thought, you have a scar too." She couldn't control herself. She kissed it lightly.

Oliver tipped his head toward her face. "Poe, you're turning me on."

"I'm not trying to." She stepped backwards, pretending she hadn't felt anything. She clasped her hands together. Sweat slid down the back of her neck. She hoped Oliver didn't see her reaction, but she was just fooling herself. Her knew her well enough to know she couldn't resist him.

Oliver grinned. He closed the gap between them, their bottom halves almost pressed together. He undressed her with his eyes for a long second. "I want you," Oliver pleaded, tilting his head to her lips.

Poe's heart raced. She shouldn't let this happen. Just before his lips brushed hers, the two of them heard someone approaching the kitchen. Oliver sighed, ran his hand through his hair, and moved away.

Lily walked in. "So, what are your plans today, Poe?"

Poe tried to compose her voice. "I'm taking Raven to the pier, then to the mall."

Lily placed her house key on the table. "This is for you. I'm going to work soon, and I get off at 8. Please be here, so I can get inside."

OLIVER FROWNED AT HIS mom. "You work today?"

"That's what I just said, dear. I know it's hard for you to pay attention to anyone besides Poe, but please try." His mom loved to tease people. It was her way of showing love and affection, just like Poe. Six years ago, his mom had picked on him that Poe was the one. He would blush, letting everyone know it was true, which his girlfriend at the time didn't appreciate. At first, Poe would nonchalantly change the subject, but eventually she began to play along.

Like today.

Poe smiled. "Can you blame him?"

Oliver felt the back of his neck flush. He knew where this was headed; the two special women in his life were on the verge of tag teaming him.

"So, who's your favorite dish partner?" Lily asked her son. Oliver looked at Poe.

"You, of course, I can never beat you, Lily," Poe answered for him. He was grateful because he couldn't just chose one—he'd always pick both.

His mom smiled and shared a look with Oliver. She examined Poe's finger, shook her head, and covered her mouth to hide a giggle.

Oh no. We're busted.

"You two honestly just made my day. Well, I'm jumping in the shower, then I'll skedaddle. Don't do anything I wouldn't do, lovebirds," his mom added before leaving the kitchen.

Poe frowned. "Lovebirds?" She stepped away from Oliver and stared at the dish she was drying.

"Mom was teasing, like usual...even though the thought isn't so far-fetched. I mean look what happened last night."

"She doesn't know what happened last night."

Oliver sighed. Everything was going well a minute ago. What had changed? Why was Poe distancing herself again? He tapped his foot on the mat. "Even Raven knows there's something between us. This morning she excused me of stealing you away from her."

Poe's body seemed to grow tense. "She said that?"

"Yeah, she said you were supposed to sleep in her room last night, and that tonight I better let that happen."

"Well then." Poe laughed, walking away. "I better go to Raven now, stealer."

"Hey, you're just trying to get out of washing dishes."

Oliver finished the dishes and didn't hear Poe for a while, so he decided to go check on her. He knocked on the bathroom door, but didn't wait for a response before he opened it. Steam and heat blasted his face. He couldn't see his reflection in the mirror. Poe's clothes were neatly folded on the top of the toilet lid with her towel hanging over the bathtub bar.

"Hello?" Poe said.

"It's me." Oliver leaned on the sink. If he saw Poe naked, he wouldn't be able to stop himself from making love to her again.

"What's up, stealer?"

"Are we cool?"

"Yeah, I mean...yeah. Considering."

Oliver rubbed his forehead. "Considering what?" He felt that time was too short to keep messing things up with her, to keep acting like an idiot around her.

"Well...I mean, we haven't talked in so long, so I didn't know how things would be between us when I got here. I didn't know if you'd avoid me or whatever...I think we're cool. But...since you have to ask, maybe I'm wrong." Poe turned the shower off and reached her hand out to grab her towel. She dried off behind the curtain, her silhouette teasing Oliver senseless.

"You thought I'd be mean to you?" he asked. The last thing he wanted was for Poe to think he was a douche bag.

"I didn't say that. Oliver, is this about last night? I don't even remember why I was mad to be honest with you. It was silly on my part; that's why I apologized." She stepped onto the floor. Wrapped only in a towel, she walked to the sink and stood in front of him. Their eyes locked. Blood rushed to his head. The room felt like a sauna. Oliver dripped with sweat. "You're in my way," she said.

"Sorry." He sat down on her clothes, watching as she rubbed lotion all over her legs.

Poe slid the towel off her body, and Oliver's mouth fell open. Was she inviting him to take her? Oliver glanced up at the ceiling, at the shower curtain, at the door, anywhere but Poe's perfectly shaped body, which was screaming to be touched.

Poe didn't seem like she was upset now. "I'm cool with you. I mean, I'd like to spend as much time as possible with you. Can I go to the pier and shopping too?"

"If you want."

Oliver paused. "Do you want me to?"

"Yes, I want to spend time with you," Poe hesitated. "How about this? If I ever want you to leave me alone, then the code words can be 'stay the hell away from me, asshole.' I doubt I'll ever have to say this, but just in case." Poe grinned. "What will your code phrase be for me?"

"I would never ask you to leave me alone."

She sighed. "Then pretend."

"I don't know." Why should he come up with phrases to keep her away? That's the last thing he wanted. Maybe she didn't want his company, and joking about it was the only way she felt comfortable expressing it to him. This thought stung a little.

"Fine then. It can be 'stay the hell away from me, bitch.' I am a bitch, so you may actually have to use this once in a while." Poe smiled, but he didn't. "Oliver, lighten up. Please."

He leaned closer to Poe and pressed his forehead against hers. It took everything for him not to kiss her. He took her hands in his. "Just promise me that if I do something to upset you, you'll let me know, so we can fix it sooner than later."

"I will, as long as you do the same."

Oliver closed his eyes. Yes, he definitely planned to do that. It was too early now; he'd have to wait a little while.

Chapter Ten

The elevator stopped, and a young couple got in with Oliver. He backed up against the wall, allowing the guy to push his floor button. The couple stood on the other side of the elevator, holding hands. They started making out. Oliver tried to give them privacy, but they were not respecting his space. He imagined it would turn into a porno within minutes, with the slow, classical music as the background. The security guard would probably enjoy the footage.

The elevator stopped again, and his neighbor, Melinda, stepped on. They exchanged smiles to each other, as she squeezed in next to him. The couple didn't notice. They hadn't stopped their make-out session. The guy had his girl pinned against the wall, rubbing her breasts. It reminded Oliver of making love to Poe the night before.

Melinda looked over. "Wow, I need a boyfriend," she whispered. Oliver laughed nervously. Did she really have a crush on him? Maybe Poe was right.

When the elevator stopped again, it was for their floor. Oliver stepped off with Melinda. She had a habit of visiting her sister on the floor right below, using the elevator instead of taking the stairs. They were twins, who had graduated with Jenna and him. "Being lazy again, huh?" Oliver teased.

"Have to be. You have no idea what fun presents itself in the elevator." She pointed to the couple, who were still going at it hot and heavy when the doors closed. "Exhibit A." Melinda patted Oliver on the back, sadness in her eyes. "Sorry about Jenna."

"Thank you." He watched her walk away, frowning. The light in the hallway flickered on and off. It never did that before; either it needed a new light bulb, or Jenna was present. Oliver doubted the second option since a chill didn't go down his spine.

He turned and saw Kate, standing in front of his door with her arms folded across her chest. She sneered and her cheeks seemed painted with an angry red. Had she stood there all night?

He approached her.

"I see your fan club keeps growing," she said. "Me, Poe, now her."

Oliver sighed. "What do you want?"

"I want to talk to you."

"If I say no, will you leave?"

"No."

"Then come in." Oliver killed with kindness. Like usual, his key got stuck. He jiggled it for a good two minutes, then the door finally opened. He let Kate enter first, then he shut the door behind them.

Kate studied him, glaring. "I see you're doing the walk of shame."

Oliver looked down at the same clothes he wore yesterday. "Are you going to keep taking jabs at me, or do you really want to talk?"

"I want to talk." She put her hands on her hips. Not really a gesture to show she was ready to talk, more like ready to kill.

Oliver sat on the couch while she stood. He refused to raise his voice. He refused to let her get the best of him. The sooner he'd let Kate vent, scream, or whatever—the sooner Oliver could be where he really wanted to be.

She strode to his coffee table and sat down on it, facing him. She leaned towards him and squeezed her eyes tightly. He knew he was in for another Oscar performance.

"It hurt so much that you left me at Ruby Tuesday's, but I understand why you did it. I let my jealousy get in the way instead of being there for you, and I'm disgusted with myself. I am so sorry, Honey. So sorry...and I'd also like to say sorry to Poe." Kate took a deep breath. "She didn't do anything wrong yesterday. It was all me."

Wow, he didn't see that coming. "I'm sorry too. I was frustrated with you, but that's no excuse for what I did. I shouldn't have left you in that parking lot. I should've taken you home, or at least called later to make sure you made it home safely."

In hindsight, Oliver understood why Kate was jealous of Poe, but she had gone overboard with it. Poe didn't do anything wrong; it was all him. He was the one drawn to her the moment he saw her at the airport. He was the one who expected them to just start where they left off. He was the one who couldn't keep his eyes off her. No wonder Kate had snapped.

"It's just...I love you." She lowered her eyes to the floor. "Did you sleep with Poe?"

Oliver's silence told her everything she needed to know. Kate sighed. She drew closer and grabbed his hands. Tears fell down her cheeks.

Oliver frowned. "Kate—"

"I love you, Honey. I forgive you. Last night meant nothing. You'll see; we'll get through this."

"Kate—"

"Honey, I don't care if you slept with her. I don't care if you sleep with her again." Oliver flinched. This wasn't the Kate he knew. "She leaves soon, so do what you have to do. Then, she'll be gone, out of your system, and we can go back to the way things were...we can go back to you giving me a key and having a future together."

"I'm sorry. I'm not the type of guy to take a break from my girlfriend to screw someone else, then take my girlfriend back." No. He was the type to just dump them. Didn't make it any better, but Oliver couldn't help it. He had to follow his heart.

Kate pouted. "What are you saying, Honey?"

Oliver took a deep breath. "I'm saying it's over between us."

Wide-eyed, she squeezed his hands. "No, no, no. You don't mean that. I love you. I'm willing to give you all the things you want. She's not. She's going to hurt you again."

"I'm sorry." Oliver closed his eyes and slouched down into his seat. Poe hadn't promised anything. Hell, he didn't even know if she wanted anything to do with him at all. He rested his head back on the couch to avoid looking at Kate, but she wouldn't let go of his hands. He hated himself for having to do this to her.

"No, I don't accept that."

"You have to."

Kate whispered, "Did you ever love me?"

He looked at her. "I care for you."

"This can't be happening! Please, Honey!" Kate freed his hands and slid her palm up his thigh. "Fuck her while she's here; I don't care. Just tell me next week we can go back to being normal. You'll love me. You'll see." She rubbed the front of his pants. He pushed her hand away, but she jumped on top of Oliver and kissed him, his lips tensed in a thin line.

"Kate, no." He tried to push her off, but she fell back in his lap. "KATE, STOP!" Oliver stood up, but she clung to him, ripping his shirt halfway off his chest.

Kate collapsed to the floor on her knees and stared up at him. "You're such a fucking fool! She's going to hurt you—she doesn't love you the way I do!" Her voice quivered, her mascara running down her face. "She's going to turn you down, then you'll be begging like a little bitch, like you made me resort to." She gave an eerie grin, her eyes wild with hope. "And, I can't wait for that moment. I may not be there, but I'll feel it in my heart!" Kate stood up and ran her fingers over her outfit to smooth it out. She swung her hair and walked towards the door. She opened it and turned around. "Karma's a bitch, you fucking fool!" She slammed the door. Oliver sprinted to lock it.

Chapter Eleven

Poe and Raven sat on the edge of the narrow pier with their legs dangling off the side. The pier was crowded with people on both sides. Poe didn't pay attention to any of them. Her main focus was on the modest sailboats and gigantic yachts that floated past. She smiled because this had been her and Jenna's favorite spot to hang out on the weekends. Even though they had loved the men in their lives, it didn't stop them from checking out eye candy, the young, hot sailors. Jenna's philosophy had been "it's okay to look as long as there's no touching involved."

One time Poe and Jenna had talked their way onto a yacht belonging to a rich couple. They sailed out to the middle of the ocean and drank margaritas, laid out in the sun, and scuba dived. Luckily they weren't a weird couple who liked swapping or swinging. All Poe and Jenna needed to do was keep giving out compliments—that couple was very narcissistic.

Poe's thoughts were interrupted when someone tapped her on the shoulder. She jumped. Oliver wouldn't have tapped her on the shoulder unless he was in a silly mood and wanted to play 'guess who.' She turned to see a woman in her twenties.

"Excuse me, ma'am. Can you tell me how to get to the pier?" She bit down on her lower lip covered with magenta lip gloss. She wore a bikini top and white spandex booty shorts.

Ma'am. Really? Poe couldn't be that much older than her; there was respecting elders, then there was being obnoxious. Poe hoped she didn't look as old as she felt. "You're already here."

"Oh, my bad. I thought there was more to it, like restaurants or shops. I'm from Ocean City, Maryland, so when I hear about boardwalks, I think the whole nine yards."

Poe smiled weakly. This pier didn't provide shops or anything, just a long, wooden plank. She could understand the girl's disappointment. "That's okay.

Hope you enjoy it." Poe wanted to tell her that it wasn't safe giving out personal information like where she lived, so besides enjoying the scenery, she should also become wiser.

The girl walked away. Raven grabbed Poe's shirt, shifting it to the left side of her body. Good thing she wasn't wearing a low-cut top, or her breasts would've been exposed. "Poe, that shirt is cool. Lookey." Raven pointed in the opposite direction of where they were sitting.

Poe turned around for a split second, not really looking at anything. "Yep, it's cool." Where was Oliver? He had discussed meeting them there after he took a quick shower. Maybe he'd changed his mind.

Raven sat criss-cross with her back to the ocean. She focused on all the tourists walking by and kept pointing out their clothing choices. She asked Poe why a person wore that particular outfit, like Poe was a mind reader. If Poe could read peoples' minds, she wouldn't waste it on fashion advice.

Poe thought if she was asked one more question about a stranger's shirt, she would scream. "Raven, do you want to draw the pretty boats?"

"No."

She sighed. "Well, do you want to watch *me* draw the pretty boats?"

"Yes." Raven turned around, so she could sit in the same direction as Poe. She dug into her purse to retrieve her mini-sketchpad and pencils, and Raven oohed and aahed. Raven leaned over Poe's left arm, and stuck her head in the way.

Poe laughed to herself. The little diva wasn't so bad after all. She was chill for a toddler. *Are four-year olds considered toddlers?* She was impressed that Raven sat still; yes, she was talkative, but so what? At least she didn't run around with Poe having to chase her. At least Raven wasn't hanging over the edge of the pier, trying to jump into the water.

Poe drew a sailboat in the water on a sunny day, then traced it with a black felt pen. Sketching was her comfort zone. She was happy to be sharing this moment with Raven because it reminded her of all the times Jenna had complimented her artwork.

"Can—can I have it?"

"Sure." Poe tore the page out and handed it to her.

She held it like a first prize winner. "Thank you. It's so pre—pretty."

Poe smiled. "You're pretty too."

"No, you're pretty." Raven wrapped her arm around Poe's arm. "Ollie says—Ollie says you're beautiful."

"Really? What does he say about Kate?"

"Ollie says that Kate is pretty. She's high maintenance and a drama queen. Ollie says she smells like strawberries. Poe, how can someone—someone smell like strawberries?"

Did Oliver really say all of that to Raven? She must have overheard him talking to Dominic and Jenna. Either way, Poe appreciated the heads up.

"Poe?"

"Yes."

"Please teach—teach me pronouns."

Like a teacher, she told her young student everything she could think of in the subject of English. Raven paid attention to every word. Just then, Poe received a text from her sister asking her to call when she wasn't busy.

After one ring, Keisha picked up. "What's up, Sis?"

"You tell me. You're the one who asked me to call."

"I'm just checking up on ya. How you holding up?"

"I'm okay...How are you?"

"I'm sure you're not okay, but I'll let that answer slide for now."

Poe rolled her eyes. Keisha was the only one who called her out on her responses on how she felt. It's not that Poe didn't trust people. She didn't want to burden anyone with her troubles. She didn't want to be the Negative Nancy of the group. "I swear I am. I even watched Raven last night, and I'll keep her for a couple more nights as well."

Keisha gasped. Just because Poe didn't want children didn't mean she couldn't be around them. She was tired of people acting like she was heartless. Before she could defend herself, Oliver walked up and handed Poe a daisy, her favorite flower.

"Thank you." She put a strand of hair behind her ear. This was why she continually kept falling back in love with him. "Oliver's here now." He sat down beside Poe. Their shoulders brushed. Raven jumped on his lap. She extended her leg into Poe's lap; Poe smiled as she patted it.

"Seems like he can't stay away from you," Keisha said.

"Don't read into it too much. He just wants to make sure I don't hurt his little cousin." Poe laughed and looked at Oliver. "Keisha says hi."

Oliver waved. "Hi, Keisha."

"Can you be alone for a minute?" her sister asked.

"Can you watch Raven for a minute or two, three, four, fifty, sixty?" Poe teased. She felt like a dork acting silly in front of him, but he made her nervous. He nodded. She thanked him by kissing him on the cheek.

She strolled up the boardwalk, accidentally bumping into an older guy, who gave her the middle finger. Poe smirked and kept moving. *Oliver gave me my favorite flower. Maybe I shouldn't push him away.* She thought of Kate. *May the best woman win.*

A handsome, younger guy turned to face her. He smiled and raised an eyebrow. She returned the same greeting, then looked away. She didn't have time to flirt.

Poe found an empty spot in the parking lot. "What's up?"

"Please don't be mad. Leo called me this morning to ask about everyone in Rhode Island. He asked about Jenna, Lily, and Oliver."

Poe frowned. "Oh well."

"I'm sorry. I thought he already knew that you were staying at Oliver's mother's house, which was idiotic on my part. I should've known you would hold back on everything. You always do."

Poe rolled her eyes. "Anyways, did he seem mad?"

"No, not really, but it seemed like he had an ah-ha moment, ah-ha my stupid ass should've went with her."

"I asked him not to come." Poe tugged at her WVU t-shirt that suddenly seemed suffocating. *Pushing people away should be my middle name.*

"Then a light bulb definitely went off. Oh my goodness, he could be on his way now."

"You really think so?" She didn't have the time or energy to keep Leo company, mourn her best friend, and deal with her best friend's family. Plus, it wouldn't be good for Oliver and Leo to meet.

"No, but I think it would mean a lot to him if you'd call him," Keisha said.

"He wasn't himself this morning." She sighed. "I'll call him, but not now."

Poe described Leo's outburst to her sister. Keisha said, "So...you and Oliver are hanging out? I know you're happy to be talking again."

"Why, yes I am." Poe knew where this conversation was headed. Her sister would want all the details, so she gave her bits and pieces to satisfy her thirst.

Keisha was amazed to hear that Oliver broke up with his girlfriend the day Poe arrived. But not as shocked as Poe had been.

"Oh my gosh, you two are so cute. Please, please, please talk to him about staying in touch after it's all said and done. And, I know it may be tempting to hook up at some point, but you two shouldn't. You're both vulnerable right now, and it's a recipe for disaster unless you both decide to make a long distance relationship work."

Poe swallowed. There was silence on both ends of the phone. *Where was this girl advice yesterday?*

"Wait a minute," Keisha said. "I know you two haven't already hooked up."

Poe bit her bottom lip. "Huh?"

"Don't you 'huh' me, young lady," Keisha imitated their mom's voice. "No more sex until you talk, okey dokey?"

"No more sex period. I know Oliver; he doesn't go for casual. I made a mess of things." A frown formed on Poe's lips. "Good thing I leave on Thursday. Can you pick me up at the airport?"

You're both vulnerable right now, and it's a recipe for disaster. Just when Poe was ready to let her guard down to see how things could progress with Oliver, her sister knocked her back to reality.

"Yes, of course, I can. Hey, don't beat yourself up. It's on Oliver too. He knows better. Don't feel guilty, Sis. Like I said, you're feeling vulnerable, so you get a pass this week, up to a month at least."

"Up to a month? I need more time than that."

"Okay, up to six months. You do self-sabotage a lot. I swear you need therapy or an ass beating," Keisha teased before they hung up.

Poe turned to face the water. It was either now or never to hear how Oliver really felt about her. If she had to, she could let him go, as long as he was happy and remained friends with her. Why did life have to be so hard? She wondered how long despair would cloud her judgment. A couple of days? A month? Six months? Could anyone really put a timeline on someone's grieving process?

Since Oliver and Raven hadn't moved, it was easy for Poe to find them. She sat down far enough away that if they wanted to touch, they'd have to stretch their arms.

"Poe, I told Ollie everything I learned—learned about pronouns. Everything. I was—was a good teacher."

A weak smile formed on Poe's lips. She gave Raven a high-five, then glanced back towards the ocean, and wiped a tear from her eye.

Oliver rubbed her shoulder. Poe looked at him and mouthed, "I'm fine. Can we talk later?"

He nodded.

Raven talked about how lucky she was to have the picture drawn of the boat. She talked about hanging it up on her wal,l like her mommy used to do. Poe promised to keep drawing Raven anything she wanted. Raven clapped in glee and jumped up; in the process, the daisy fell off her lap and landed in the water. "Oh no, am I in trouble?" she whispered.

"No, it's okay."

Raven pouted. "I'm sorry."

"It's okay. I can get another daisy," Poe said. Raven gave her a hug. She met Oliver's gaze.

What could've been if Poe would've waited to make love to him? They could've talked, laid all their emotions out on the table, then from there decided if they should get back together or not. Now, he'd probably hate her if she asked for a friendship.

For whatever reason, Raven didn't let go from the embrace, so they both held each other. Poe rubbed Raven's back and closed her eyes. She pushed confusion aside and felt at peace. Whatever would happen, would happen. Easier said than done.

Chapter Twelve

Oliver stood behind Poe in the elevator while she held hands with Raven. He wondered what Poe wanted to talk about. Usually when a woman asked to talk, it meant bad news was coming. He couldn't bear any more. Just being a few feet away from Poe made him crave her. There was no way to shut those feelings off. He had to convince her to give him a second chance.

The door opened and a man, woman, and little girl squeezed into the elevator with them. Oliver tilted his head and smiled at the family. The little girl, no more than two-year old, was cute in her *Dora the Explorer* outfit. She waved at Raven. His little cousin could use a friend, someone who was real instead of imaginary. Oliver thought he would've had a daughter or son by now, but it wasn't in the cards for him just yet.

The little girl grinned at Oliver, and he waved. Poe looked straight ahead, not paying any attention to the family. Maybe she was nervous about entering his apartment. Before she left, it used to be her place as well. It should spring happy memories, all the fun times they had together. Oliver felt this was exactly what Poe needed.

He placed his hand on her back, and her entire body tensed. They got out on his floor. Oliver was nervous that Kate would be waiting for him, but thankfully, she wasn't. How Poe had talked this morning, she probably would've invited her in.

His key didn't stick this time, as though the apartment welcomed him inside. Even his place knew Poe belonged there. Raven went to the bathroom, and Poe followed. Shortly after, Poe walked out, leaving the door open a crack.

Oliver lounged on the couch. Instead of approaching him, Poe browsed the books on his mini-bookshelf. She smiled at the collection of her comic books, *Pittsburgh's World*, running her finger over every issue. "I didn't know you had these."

Oliver snuck up behind her. "Yep, I have every issue. I'm very proud of you." He kissed her on the cheek.

"That's why I have to be at work Monday morning; its the deadline to show my editor my work, and Tuesday it'll go into production. Then, you can add an extra book to your shelf."

He gazed into her weary eyes. "Can I ask you something?"

Poe nodded.

Oliver wasn't arrogant or cocky. In fact, usually he could use a self-esteem boost, so it flattered him to think Poe based one of the characters in her comic on him. And one on her. In fact, their relationship as a whole. "Am I Malcolm?"

Poe blushed. "Yes."

Oliver's heart thumped in his chest. She'd wanted to share their love with the world. This gave him hope that she still felt the same way.

They smiled at each other. He moved a lock of hair behind her ear. They stared at each other for a long second. If Raven wasn't with them, they would make love on the couch or floor because they wouldn't make it to his bedroom. That's exactly why he could never be Poe's friend.

He leaned in to kiss her, but she pushed him away. Frustrated, he leaned again. She took a step backward. "We can't...Oliver, I leave Thursday."

"What?" Oliver's voice cracked a little.

"I leave Thursday." She shut her eyes. She had never liked to see him hurt.

He dropped to his knees, then slumped back against his bookshelf. "But you just said you work on Monday. I thought you leave this weekend."

"I was but—"

"But what?" Oliver studied her face, but Poe avoided his gaze. He scooted closer to her. *Please talk to me.*

"The plans changed. I tried, but all the flights are either booked or non-existent. This was the only one I could pick where I wouldn't go over Monday morning. I'm sorry; I tried—"

"Poe," Raven screamed through the crack in the door.

Poe turned to go, but Oliver grabbed her hand. "Poe."

"We'll talk later." She shook her hand away, but he wouldn't let go. Those three words gutted him.

Poe raised his hand and shyly kissed it. Oliver groaned, mesmerized by her brown eyes. There was a hint of guilt in them. "Oliver, we'll talk later."

He let her go and watched her walk away. Oliver, breathing heavy, slammed his fist on top of the bookshelf.

"SORRY YOU WASTED TIME coming to the mall. Let me give you gas money," Poe offered.

Oliver shook his head. "I don't want your money."

"Why? It's not counterfeit." She fidgeted in the passenger seat, staring out the window.

By the time they had arrived in the parking lot, Raven was sound asleep in the back seat. All Poe wanted was a new sketchbook and mystery novel from the bookstore but didn't feel right having to wake Raven up. She had accompanied Keisha on plenty of shopping trips where her little niece, LaToya, would throw temper tantrums because of lack of sleep. Poe wasn't in the mood for that today.

As if sensing her agitation, Oliver frowned. "Are you okay? Maybe you're hungry. Tell me where you want to go, and I'll take you." He stepped on the gas pedal when the light turned green at the four-way intersection near his old high school. It was the central focal point of his hometown.

Poe sighed. "Stop being so nice all the time."

Keisha's advice had run through her mind all day, entering Oliver's apartment had done a number on her, all the memories rushing back at once. She hadn't had time to process it all. Poe had expected to see Kate's influence all over the apartment—new furniture, her clothes everywhere, maybe a centerpiece on his table, but there had been no signs of Kate at all. The apartment was exactly the same as before she left, and that freaked Poe out. She couldn't start over with Oliver. Not when they both wanted different things. It was like being tempted to open Pandora's Box without considering the consequences first. Like the consequences of breaking her ex's heart again.

Oliver halted at a stop sign, then turned left, heading towards his neighborhood.

"I'm not hungry." She lowered her gaze. "Why did you give me a daisy today?"

"Do I need a reason to give you a flower?" Oliver tried to sound charming, but it didn't work. "I wanted to make you smile, and...Kate was at my place, so we talked right before I got to the pier. Nothing happened, but she—"

"You don't have to explain anything. We're not together."

"Poe—"

"It's fine that you talked to her." She smiled weakly. "You should work things out."

He frowned. "What?"

"You heard me. I didn't stutter. I talked to Leo this morning."

"Leo?"

"Yes, you know my boyfriend. That's what couples do—they talk. They definitely don't leave the people they love out in parking lots." Poe flinched, knowing she hit below the belt.

Oliver gave her an icy stare, and his hands gripped tighter on the steering wheel.

She sighed. "He told me I'm not the motherly type at all."

"Well, you're doing fine with Raven," Oliver said calmly, as though he was incapable of arguing with her.

"Yeah right. I suck with kids." She glanced out the window. "That's why we broke up in the first place."

"Poe—"

"If we hadn't slept together last night, would you even be talking to me right now?" She thought about her sister's warning again. Granted, she probably should have been gentler with the approach, but she was on the defense. He was the reason she had been nervous to arrive in Rhode Island in the first place.

Poe wiped her tears away, not wanting Oliver to see her cry. She gripped her arms around her body. She couldn't bring herself to look at him.

He was the one who refused to talk to her for a year and had the nerve to act like nothing had changed. He had made her feel low and worthless, but now, he wanted to be her knight-in-shining-armor. Well, how many times was he Kate's knight-in-shining-armor before he left her with no explanation? If he could do that to Kate, then he could do it to her as well. And, Poe wouldn't stand for that.

OLIVER'S HEART SANK when Poe said they weren't together. Not knowing how to answer, he remained silent.

Poe folded her arms across her chest. "Well."

"That's really what you think of me?" Oliver rolled down his window, hoping some fresh air would help his car seem less boxed in. He snuck a peak at Poe, then quickly returned his attention to the road.

"It's not like it's so far-fetched. You haven't talked to me in a year, Oliver. In a year! So yes, I do question your motives for being around me. Answer me this, when I get home, will you talk to me? Will you be my friend?"

Oliver cracked his knuckles, then quickly put his hands back on the steering wheel. He shook his head. "I can't be friends with you." *Friends don't make love. Friends aren't in love with each other.*

"That's good to know. If you can't talk to me when I'm not here, then don't talk to me now. Just leave me alone. I leave in two days, then you can go back to acting like I don't exist."

"Poe—"

Poe slouched down into her seat. "Please leave me alone, Oliver." She sobbed with her arms wrapped around herself.

Oliver tried to concentrate on the road. He didn't know what to say, and even if he did, she wouldn't allow him to explain. He drove slower than normal, sometimes drifting off the road when he glanced over at Poe.

Except for the soft snoring of Raven, a heavy silence filled the car. Oliver's cheeks flushed red. He had said from the beginning that he wanted Poe, that he wanted to get back together. If she didn't want that, she should have spoken up. He refused to be her jump-off or fuck buddy.

Oliver clenched the steering wheel as he sped up. He needed to cool off. He turned up the volume on the radio and stared straight ahead.

Finally, they pulled up at his mom's house. Oliver decided it'd be better to bring Poe there than his place. He had no idea what was wrong with her—she was starting to act as hysterical as Kate, and it scared him.

He turned the engine off. Poe opened her door and shut it, as though this was the last place she wanted to be. "I'll get Raven," he said.

"No, I got her," she said, opening the back door.

"Poe, come on. Don't be like this." She avoided his gaze, and that was killing him. He'd rather she yell at him than give him nothing at all.

She managed to pick Raven up, but struggled to shut the door. Oliver walked over, but Poe shrugged away his help. "You're the one making this an all or nothing situation, so like you, I choose nothing."

He shoved both hands in his pockets. "You don't mean that."

"It's so easy for you to dismiss people, so I figure I'll give it a try." Poe met his gaze, her eyes determined. "I mean it, leave me alone, Oliver. It's for the best." She carried Raven into the house and didn't even glance back at him.

Reluctantly, Oliver opened his car door. He punched the steering wheel until he hurt his hand, then he slumped over it, burying his head into his arms. He had to make things right with Poe; he couldn't live without her. He sat in his car for a long time, feeling disoriented, then he drove off.

WHEN RAVEN WOKE UP from her nap, she rambled about her favorite television shows as Poe used her fork to play with her food. She wasn't hungry, yet stayed in the kitchen to keep Raven company. She gave the occasional nod, pretending to pay attention.

Poe was still processing being in Jenna's old room when she had tucked Raven into bed. The room had been the same, like she never left. There were red walls and black furniture. Jenna had painted a huge family tree on the wall facing the window. All the MacNamara's names were written in Goth-like font. Jenna had been obsessed with her genealogy. Would Raven obsess over it too? Or would the tradition die with Jenna?

Poe avoided the anxiety by working on her comic book. Oliver tried to call and text her. Her only reply, *Leave me alone*. Jenna had been Poe's only friend, who actually knew everything about her and Oliver. She had tried many times to make things better between them, but it wasn't meant to be. Oliver wanted everything perfect, in an order. Wife, children, happy life. Poe wanted freedom. They were like two ends of a road.

Instead of dealing with her ex, Poe had decided to call Leo and apologize. She needed to focus on her present, not her past. Oliver wouldn't want anything to do with her once she left, so she had to deal with it.

Knock. Knock.

Poe jumped up. "Raven, I'll be right back."

"Okay. Hurry back; I have to tell you the sound cows make."

Poe paused at the front door. "Who is it?"

A female voice answered, "Your favorite person."

Poe mustered a smile and opened the door to greet Lily. "I fixed dinner. Please eat, so it doesn't go to waste."

When they reached the kitchen, Raven had a twinkle in her eye. "Hi, Aunt Lily. Mmmm, this food is so delicious. Wanna know how much?"

"How much?" Lily looked at Raven.

"It's so del—delicious that I'm scarfing it down." Raven grinned at Poe.

"Well, let me get a plate then." Lily went to the stove and fixed her plate. Poe sat down, pretending to finish her macaroni and cheese. "Poe, we should go to our favorite café before you leave."

"I'd like that. Thursday morning?"

Lily nodded and took her seat.

Poe grabbed her cell phone and logged onto Facebook. She changed her status to, *I miss my best friend Jenna (RIP)*. She sighed, closing her eyes. She thought of Dominic. Yesterday, he had called his daughter, but today he didn't. "I'll be right back," she excused herself.

She made her way to the bedroom and slowly closed the door. She settled in a chair and dialed Dominic's number. It rang three times. *Why isn't he picking up? Where is he?* "Pick up. Pick up. Pick up."

"Hey, Poe," his voice sounded rough, like he'd been crying.

"Hey, Dominic, how are you?" A silly question. Of course, he's not well the night before Jenna's funeral. Poe wished she had a rewind button to ask a more appropriate question.

"Been better. What's up?"

"I was worried about you since I haven't heard from you all day. I'm sorry that I've hardly spent time with you since I got here. I um...I want to be here for you. You're one of my best friends." Poe wiped sweat from her forehead. "I'm not good with stuff like this, and I know you already have a lot on your plate, but please tell me what I can do to help you, to help you feel a tiny bit better."

"Taking care of my daughter is enough. I should go."

"Wait. Do you want to talk to Raven?"

"I can't. Tell her Daddy loves her." His voice was somber and defeated.

"Tell her yourself, Dominic. You can tell her tomorrow."

"I'm not myself."

"No one expects you to be. You just lost your wife; someone should be there for you." Poe shot up from her seat. "I'll come over."

"No don't, just keep Raven safe. I just...I just need sleep. I'll sleep and things will get better. I got to go, Poe."

"Dominic, please call me if you need to talk. I don't care how late it is."

"Goodbye." Dominic hung up the phone. That wasn't like him at all; he sounded like a pod person.

Poe dialed Oliver's cell phone, biting her fingernail.

"Poe, I—"

"Oliver, listen to me. I may be overreacting, but it's better safe than sorry. Please go to Dominic's and check on him. He said he wasn't himself, like it was a warning. Please, Oliver." Poe forced back tears.

"I'm on my way."

Her body trembled as she paced the room. She wasn't sure if she should call 911. She tried to calm herself down. She didn't want Raven to find her like this.

Chapter Thirteen

Oliver knocked on the door, trying to keep his fear in check. Dominic didn't answer. Oliver looked around the porch for a hidden key, frantically searching under the welcome mat, but to no avail. "Shit." He picked up the plant but didn't find a key underneath it. He knocked on the door again. Still no answer. A chill ran down his spine. "Dominic!" Oliver jiggled the door knob and was surprised when it turned.

He opened the door with caution, hoping that Poe had just overreacted.

The house was pitch black. Oliver felt along the wall and switched on the light. He jumped when he saw Dominic sitting on the couch staring into nothingness. *What is it about couches, living rooms, and depression?*

Dominic did not acknowledge his presence. He didn't blink, and he didn't turn his head. Oliver walked slowly to the couch and picked up the bottle of liquor, and container of sleeping pills. He sat beside Dominic, examining the bottle. It was still quite full. Oliver sighed in relief and set the stuff on the floor. "Dominic." Oliver stared at him, but he was still in a daze.

"Poe called you, huh? I figured I scared her." There was no emotion in his voice. "That makes her a good friend. She was right; I wanted to take those pills and drown my sorrow in Vodka. I haven't slept in over two nights. Do you know how awful that feels?" Dominic spoke, as if he were talking to himself. He turned to look at Oliver. "If I'm honest with you, will you keep it between us?"

"Of course."

"No, I mean it, just between us. You can only discuss it with me, then take it to the grave." Dominic covered his mouth with his hand. "Sorry, you know what I mean."

There was an awkward silence between them.

"Yeah, I know. It'll be our secret," Oliver promised.

"I just want to sleep. I'm getting desperate, so desperate, that I was going to take as many pills as possible before I felt drowsy. And, if that didn't work, I'd try to get drunk to get sleepy that way. I was willing to take that chance," Dominic said.

Oliver got the message loud and clear; he remembered how Poe had a mini-breakdown in the bathroom. Maybe Dominic was going through this phase too. Oliver hung his head in shame and felt a knot form in his throat. He couldn't let his friend go down that road. "That's not the way to go, man. You shouldn't be alone. You should come with me to my mom's; maybe you'll feel better being near Raven or just having company. We're all dealing with this. Let's all deal together."

"You're right. Let's all deal together. Well, guess what I just found out five hours earlier?" He paused, then whispered, "My Love wasn't hit by a drunk driver. The guy was on his way to the hospital to watch his baby be born."

Oliver was shocked. Maybe he'd heard wrong.

Dominic stood up and flung the remote control, a pile of books, and a couple of wooden coasters over, causing them to crash on the floor. He reached under and flipped over his coffee table. He ripped paintings off the wall, then ran into the kitchen. Oliver heard him dragging glasses out of the cabinets, glass shattering everywhere. Then he threw pots and pans against the wall.

Oliver didn't flinch.

The killer was a drunk driver; the officer had said that for a reason. It wasn't like they were in a game and could hit the re-do button. It's not like Rhode Island cops weren't efficient. No one in his family pissed law enforcement or the hospital staff off, so this couldn't be a sick joke. Oliver refused to believe the first account was false. He would continue to believe it—anything else he'd consider a cover up, and he wasn't into conspiracy theories.

Oliver sat there like a zombie. Dominic walked out from the kitchen and stood in front of him. He glared at Oliver in defeat. "I would've flipped the couch too, but you won't get up."

"Want me to get up?"

"Only if you help me flip it."

They nodded in agreement. Oliver stood, then they walked behind the couch and lifted it. It was pretty heavy, so they grunted, their feet sliding on the wooden floor, but they finally managed to flip it. Dominic sat down on the edge of the upside-down couch and smiled weakly. "Now that's what I call male bonding."

A long silence lingered. The rooms didn't magically straighten themselves.

"...So are you coming with me to my mom's?" Oliver asked.

"I'll be fine, Oliver. Your mom doesn't need a crowded house. Trust me, I'll be fine. You can even take the pills and liquor if you don't believe me."

"I'd rather you come, though." He stuck his hands in his pockets. "Mom won't mind."

"Nah, that's okay."

"Please, Dominic. It's either come with me, or I'll spend the night here." He folded his arms across his chest.

"Not if I call the cops for trespassing." Dominic rolled his eyes. "Fine, I'll go if you wipe that look off your face. Just let me pack. You don't have to follow me to my bedroom. I won't hang myself or jump out of the window. Granted, it's a two story house, so I doubt I'd die from that anyway." He stomped up the stairs with slouched shoulders.

Oliver pulled out his cell phone and texted Poe, *We're on our way.* He walked into the kitchen to sweep up the glass. He dumped it into a paper bag and threw the contents in the trash. Then, he picked up pots and pans off the floor and placed them in the sink.

In the living room, he struggled to put the couch back in its upright position. He examined the picture frames. They had fallen, but no glass had shattered. He ran his hand over Poe's sketch, a scary pumpkin patch. He grinned.

Dominic came downstairs with a backpack. He looked around the room. "Hey man, you didn't have to do that."

Oliver shrugged his shoulders. "I didn't mind."

POE WAITED ON THE FRONT steps under the porch light. She was eager for Dominic and Oliver to arrive. She shouldn't have been so harsh in the car or when Oliver texted her hours ago, but she felt it'd be easier to let him go if they didn't communicate. She was so confused. Did she really just want a one-night stand? Or did she want something more? It didn't matter because Oliver wouldn't even give her a second thought once she left for Pittsburgh. At least he came through with helping Dominic tonight, just like she knew he would.

A chill went down her spine when Oliver's car pulled up to the curb. She jumped up and stretched her legs. There were no streetlights, but Poe could see the outlines of two men. She couldn't hear them though. They were huddled together, like they were sharing a secret.

Dominic neared the porch. "You mad at me?" Poe asked, reaching to hug him.

"No, you did what you had to do. I can respect that." A weak smile formed on Dominic's lips. Poe noticed his eyes were bloodshot red, sunken in, and he had wrinkles on his forehead.

What had the guys talked about tonight? "Well, just so you know I didn't let Lily know I suspected anything wrong, so—"

"Good. Good. There's no need to worry her. I'll be fine; we'll all be fine. It'll take time, but we'll get there."

Fine. Fine. Fine. Does Dominic really believe that? Silence lingered, and Poe swallowed nervously. She wanted to ask what had happened back at his house, but she decided not to press the issue. She thought he'd like to hear about his daughter, maybe that would help him feel better. "Raven's already taken a bath, and I read her a bedtime story. But, she's not tired yet. She's in there watching *The Lion King.*"

Poe tried not to pay attention to Oliver, to prove that she meant it shouldn't be all or nothing. But, it took all of her strength not to walk over to him and wrap her body into his.

Dominic patted Poe's shoulder. "Now, that I'm here, I see you're trying to be absolved of all responsibility of Raven."

"Me? Never." Poe smiled

"I'm going inside to say hello," Oliver said.

"Can you turn the porch light off," Dominic said. "So Poe and I don't get attacked by random flying bugs?"

Poe gazed into the dark street. She realized Oliver was avoiding her, but she felt she deserved it. She had done the same thing to him.

Dominic and Poe sat next to each other on the top step. They were an arm's length away, yet she felt the distance growing between them. Neither looked at each other. Dominic cleared his throat. "Remember at Summit Hall how me, you, and My Love would sit on the porch and make fun of all the drunks coming back to the dorm?"

They reminisced about their favorite moments at West Virginia University. Poe's favorite memory was when a guy almost kicked her in the forehead, then proceeded to flirt with her. Jenna had been her wing-woman. For someone who could hardly stand on his feet, the drunk guy had pretty good swagger. Dominic's favorite memory was when a huge crowd was out on the porch, then two male passersby joined them. One had gotten in a verbal fight with a resident and asked, "Hey Zack Morris, where's your gang of Screech and Lisa Turtle?" *How is there even a comeback to that?*

They laughed about their favorite moments inside Summit Hall. "Remember when me and Jenna took Ballroom Dancing? No one could stop us from practicing in the lounge," Poe said.

"No one wanted to, especially the guys. We all hoped you two would get lost in the moment and kiss."

"It's hard to get lost in the moment when all we did was laugh." Poe nudged him in a playful way. "Remember our freshmen year when you pretended to be my ex to get guys to stay away?"

He smirked. "Of course, I'll never forget that. I was your first slow dance."

Dominic had met Poe on the first day they had moved onto the seventh floor of Summit. They became best friends instantly. Poe kept mentioning how cool the guy down the hall was, so then Jenna began hanging out with them too. The three of them were inseparable on campus, and even off campus, for a good two years. Dominic and Jenna hadn't begun dating until their junior year at college.

"I thought you two were crazy for wanting to stay there after our freshmen year," Dominic said.

"And we thought you were crazy for wanting to leave."

Dominic had moved into his own apartment while the women stayed in the dorms for all four years. They loved getting maid service every two weeks; plus, their room was the biggest one on the floor with its own bathroom. It was worth staying there even though Summit Hall was located on downtown campus. The majority of Poe and Jenna's classes were on Evansdale campus, but that's what the PRT, the subway to travel between campuses, was for.

Dominic held Poe's hand and squeezed it gently. He took a deep breath. "My Love wasn't killed by a drunk driver." He paused, lowering his gaze to the ground. "He was actually rushing to the hospital to see the birth of his baby."

"What?" Poe's mouth dropped open.

"Yeah, that's what I said to the cops when they called me today. If this was a Lifetime movie, I would bring that woman flowers to make sure she and her baby were okay, then we would fall in love and call it a day," Dominic said sarcastically.

Sarcasm was his defense mechanism, like how Poe had plenty of ways to avoid tough subjects. That's why they got along so well. They could just be themselves without fearing that someone would judge them, or misunderstand them. Poe had seen enough movies to add to the topic, but she couldn't bring herself to play along. She was stunned by the news, and she couldn't handle anything else, anything deep. Would Dominic fall in love again? He was only in his late twenties, and very attractive. Poe could see women flocking to him. He had the widower and single dad vibe to his advantage. He would move on with his life while Jenna remained under ground.

It pained Poe to swallow; she felt like she had to throw up.

"I didn't want Raven to see me weak like this. I'm her dad. She's supposed to look up to me." Dominic cried on Poe's shoulders, and she needed to comfort him—someone living. She couldn't comfort her late friend no matter how much she wanted to.

Chapter Fourteen

Poe heard the front door open and shut behind her. Oliver walked to the front step of the porch, and Poe didn't turn around. She continued to stare at the shadows in the street.

Dominic stood up. "Is my sweetie still awake?"

"Yeah," Oliver answered. Dominic went inside. Oliver sat with his back against the railing, facing Poe, stretching his legs across the bottom step.

Poe shuddered; he was staring at her. His glare was so intense, so broody. "Thanks for bringing him here in one piece." She stood up.

Oliver tried to grab her hand, but she swiped it away. "Can't you stay and talk to me?"

"No, I meant what I said in the car; if it's all or nothing, I choose nothing." Poe walked to the door. She knew she was acting irrational, but she couldn't help it. She felt lost and sick to her stomach. This week was bringing out the worst in her. How could she learn to help anyone else when she didn't even know how to help herself?

"Poe, I'm sorry I hurt you. You left me, and I was hurt. I just—I couldn't talk to you because it hurt too much. You left me. I'm sorry. Please forgive me. I never wanted to hurt you. I thought you wanted me to leave you alone. I thought—it was hard, but I thought I was doing what you wanted."

Her hand fell from the knob. She covered her face and sobbed. "It's not what I wanted. Why did you think that?"

Oliver rose to his feet and leaned against the front door. Poe glanced away, avoiding his gaze. He rubbed her back. "I thought the only reason you tried contacting me was to see if I was okay. I couldn't handle that; I wasn't okay. I'm not okay without you. I love you." He leaned in towards Poe and kissed her gently, as though she would break in his arms.

Poe stepped back. "We can't...Oliver, we can't."

Oliver stepped forward. "I'm in love with you, Poe. When I said we can't be friends, I didn't mean that I don't care about you. It's the opposite. I'm *in love* with you. I'm attracted to you, and I can't turn that off. Me being with you is all that I know—I can't be your friend. When we have something real, we can't just throw it away. Please, Poe." He kissed her again, more passionately, more desperately this time.

She melted in his arms. Then, guilt sunk in. She wanted Oliver, but she knew she had to let him go. It hurt like hell, but it was for the best.

She pulled away and held his face with both of her hands. "Oliver, I'm so sorry that I hurt you when I left. I was trying to do the right thing; this relationship isn't fair to you. I don't want kids, and that's not going to change."

"But, it's okay. We don't have to have any."

She shook her head. "No, no, no. You want them."

"I want you."

"No...we can't."

"Poe, I love you. You're all that I need; I'm miserable without you. We don't have to have kids."

"No, you want them. You can't give that up for me." Poe frowned. "It's not fair to you, and it's not fair to me. You say you're okay with it, but eventually you *will* resent me. Or eventually you'll ask me to reconsider. Please let me go, Oliver. Let me go."

Poe and Oliver had been technically broken up for two years, but shortly after their first break up, he constantly pursued her. They still hooked up all the time, and they still acted like a couple but never officially said those words.

At the end of the first year, when they were in a café, she had noticed Oliver eyeing a mother with her newborn. Even though he never pressured Poe, she knew he really wanted kids. She was holding him back, and it didn't sit right with her. So, Poe moved back to her hometown and let Oliver go. He deserved happiness. He deserved everything he wanted in life.

Today, she had noticed how Oliver looked at the little girl in the elevator, and how he was so comfortable around Raven. Poe let go of his face and tried to walk away.

He grabbed her by the arm, then trapped her against the door. "I can't let you go."

"Yes, you can. You did it once, so you can do it again." Poe wiggled, but Oliver wouldn't let go.

He placed his forehead against hers. Poe closed her eyes. "Give me a chance to show you. I know you believe that actions speak louder than words, so let me show you. Let me prove it to you," he continued.

Poe was tired of fighting. What was the point if he wouldn't listen?

"I love you," he said.

"I love you too, Oliver. That's why I'm trying to do the right thing. I want you to be happy."

"Leaving me isn't the right thing. I didn't talk to you because it's what I thought you wanted. I was miserable, you were miserable. Clearly, I was in the wrong. You think leaving me is for the best, but it's not. It's not what I want. We don't have to have kids as long as I have you. That's all I need. Please believe me. We can get through this. We can get through this together—not apart."

Poe's arms ached as his grip became tighter and tighter around her. She had never seen this side of him before. "Let go of me."

He frowned. "Poe, I can't. Please. We can work this out."

"I mean let go of my arm."

Oliver glanced down at his hands then back at her. He released Poe and rubbed the back of his neck. "Sorry," he whispered.

Poe rubbed the top of her arms. "I want you in my life. That's why I was so mad when you wouldn't talk to me. I had to listen about your life through Jenna and Dominic instead of from you. It hurt, but I get it now...I leave soon. Are you asking me for a long distance relationship or—"

"I want you in my life too, in whatever way you'll have me, I'll take."

Clearly not friendship. Poe hadn't realized that Oliver still carried those deep feelings for her. She thought of Leo, who had never done anything to deserve this. Once again, she was in a predicament, and it was all her fault.

She made her way back to the steps and sat down. Oliver followed, sitting close enough to her that their thighs and shoulders brushed. "Can I ask you something?"

"Sure."

"Why did you make love to me last night?"

It would not sound good enough to say that she was caught up in the moment; that at the time, it wasn't about getting back together—it was about drifting back to familiarity. Poe couldn't tell Oliver this because she knew it would hurt him. She placed her right hand over her heart. "It felt right."

Oliver smiled, shifting his body to face her. "If we didn't make love, I would've talked to you for the rest of your stay. I hope you know that."

"I do. Why didn't you say all this in the car?"

"It's not like you gave me a chance to speak."

Poe smirked. Damn right, she had been angry. She wrapped her arms around him and put her head on his shoulder.

POE EAVESDROPPED AGAINST the bedroom door. She had wanted to say goodnight to Dominic and Raven, but she didn't want to interrupt their conversation. She should have stepped away to give them privacy, but her feet wouldn't budge.

"Is Poe my new mommy?" Raven asked.

Dominic paused. "Why do you ask that?"

"Be—because Mommy said I have two mommies, her and my godmommy."

Poe had never caught on that the little girl may be treating her differently, more respectful in a sense, trying to gain her approval. *I'm so clueless sometimes. No wonder I'm not good with kids.*

"Yes, Poe is your godmother. She is someone your mommy and I trusted to take care of you if something bad ever happened to us. So yes, you can think of her as someone important in your life."

"I love Mommy. I love you too."

"I love you too, sweetheart."

"Can I see—see Poe every single day?" Raven asked. Poe was flattered. Maybe she didn't do as bad a job of baby-sitting as she thought.

"I don't know about every single day, but we can visit her in Pittsburgh. I'm sure it's okay to keep in touch over the phone."

"Good. I'd like that. When does she leave?"

"I don't know. We'll have to ask her," Dominic replied.

"Will she dis—disappear like Mommy, and I'll never see her again?" Raven asked. Poe wiped a tear from her eye.

"You may not physically see her, but your mommy will always be in your heart...for Poe, she won't disappear forever. You'll see her again; remember we'll take trips to visit her."

"Oh I see...Daddy, even though—even though Poe is my godmommy, you can't marry her. It would hurt Ollie."

Dominic chuckled. "Don't worry. I have no intentions of hurting Ollie."

Even Raven was rooting for them to get back together. Why did Poe continue to have doubts? Why did she always have to overanalyze everything instead of follow her heart?

When everyone fell silent, Poe silently crept inside the room, and coughed to get their attention. Dominic looked up and grinned.

She smiled back. "I thought you may need this." Poe laid his overnight bag on the floor.

"Thanks," Dominic said.

Raven glanced up. "POE! When do you leave?"

"Thursday."

Raven stared at Poe intensely. She seemed to have the MacNamara family trait of being intense or broody about everything. "When's Thursday?"

"Well, you'll sleep tonight. When you wake up, it'll be Wednesday, then you'll go to sleep again. It'll be Thursday."

"I won't go—go to sleep, then Thursday won't never come."

Dominic patted Raven on the head. "It doesn't work that way, sweetheart." He explained it in terms that she could understand. Poe had known back in college that he would make a terrific father. Just like when she set eyes on Oliver, she knew he would too.

She could picture it now. She would fumble with explanations to their son or daughter, and Oliver would know the right thing to say. Would she make a good mom? Would that even matter if they had a great dad? If Oliver was willing to give up his dream to be with her, then she should consider the possibility of having a child down the line. Poe's revelation surprised her. Where did that come from?

"Well, it looks like it's your bedtime. Raven, can I have a hug?"

"YES!" Raven climbed out of bed and ran into Poe's legs.

Poe laughed and leaned down to wrap her arms around Raven. "Be good for your daddy."

"I promise I will."

Poe hugged her again, and said, "good night" to everyone. She left wondering why everyone else could express their emotions freely while she acted like a robot. Could her wall ever get knocked down?

OLIVER SAT ON THE EDGE of his mom's bed, while she lay under the covers. It wasn't like her to go to bed early. "Tomorrow's going to be a long day," he said.

"I know. I already told my manager that I may be an hour late."

He frowned, squinting his eyes. "Wait. What? You're working tomorrow?" He understood his mom working on holidays, even if it was Thanksgiving or Christmas. He understood someone going to work after attending a funeral of a person they hardly knew. He even comprehended his mom not feeling comfortable with bereavement, but he didn't get his mom now.

"Of course I am. Why wouldn't I?"

"Out of respect for Jenna."

"Me missing work isn't going to bring her back. I'll get my shit together before going in because, trust me, I'll be very sad tomorrow, but my girls need me and they are living."

Oliver didn't accept his mom's answer; he stood up and scolded her with his eyes. "Jenna will be happy to know that she's worth an extra hour of your time." He turned to walk out. "I guess when it's my time, I'll just get an hour too," Oliver said on his way out the door.

"Oliver O'Reilly MacNamara, you get back in here!"

Even though he was upset, Oliver followed orders. He stood in the doorway with his arms folded across his chest, and his foot tapping nervously.

"I plan to give you no time," she said. "No parent wants to outlive their child, so hopefully, when it's your time to go, I will be long dead." She closed her eyes for a moment, frowning. "And, when it's my time to go, I want you to live your life. I want you to celebrate the happy times we had together and not grieve the loss of me...everyone grieves in their own way, so don't you dare judge me on how I do it."

Oliver pouted and looked at the floor, like a little boy getting a lecture before receiving a time-out. "No, I don't understand it," he mumbled.

"You don't have to understand, but you should accept it."

No, I don't.

POE STOOD IN FRONT of her dresser, texting on her cell phone. Glancing up in the mirror, she caught a glimpse of Oliver behind her. "Whoa. You scared me." She spun around to face him.

Oliver leaned over her shoulder. "Who you talking to?"

Poe finished typing, *Goodnight Leo,* turned off the phone, then plugged it into the outlet. Oliver's lips were tense, his eyes narrowed, and his cheeks were rage red. *What could have possibly happened between the porch and now?* "What's wrong with you?"

"You avoiding my question is what's wrong with me."

"No, you came in here with an attitude, so I'll ask again, what's wrong with you?" If he would've appeared to be in a better mood, then she would have explained that Leo had texted her to say goodnight and to let her know that she could call if she needed him tomorrow. She had replied to be polite, but there was no way she was stating that now.

Oliver sat down on the edge of the bed and looked down at his feet. Poe braced herself. It seemed like he could break down any minute. His voice was shaky. "Mom's going to work tomorrow. She refused to call off."

Poe bit her bottom lip and ran her hand through her hair. "Will she miss Jenna's funeral?"

"No, but that's not the point." Oliver sniffed. "It's like she doesn't even care that Jenna's gone. She's treating tomorrow like any other day, and Jenna deserves better than that."

Poe bent down with her knees on the carpet, and leaned in between his legs. She placed her hands over his clenched fists. He lifted his eyes and stared at her. "Your mom's work is her comfort zone; it puts her at ease. Say tomorrow I go to the pier because it puts me at ease. I can remember the moments I had with Jenna there, so say someone wants to cry, but another person wants to laugh and remember the funny moments they shared with her...your mom knows how much Jenna was proud of her job." Poe took a deep breath. "Perhaps that's your mom's way of honoring her. People grieve in their own way. There's no right or wrong answer."

Oliver nodded his head and embraced Poe. He sobbed on her shoulder while she rubbed his back.

Chapter Fifteen

The next morning, Poe studied her reflection in the mirror and sipped her coffee. She kept sneaking peeks of Oliver sleeping on the left side of the bed. She didn't want to wake him, so she tried to be quiet as possible. To calm herself, she took deep breaths, as if she was practicing yoga or meditation. Poe had her door wide open because she wanted to hear when someone woke up. Right now, it seemed like she was the only one roaming around. Instead of time moving slowly, it moved too fast for Poe's liking. She had woken up at 6 AM. It was already two hours later.

She fidgeted with her hands. Before she knew it, she would be packed in a church surrounded by dread and people crying. She didn't know if she could handle it. She had butterflies in her stomach. If only she could find an excuse to get out of attending the funeral.

Poe listened to Oliver's quiet snoring. *Will he feel better today? Or will it be worse?* Either way, she planned to support him.

She thought of potential endings for her comic strip. It had to end in a cliffhanger, so her readers would be motivated to buy the next one. Her daydreaming was a way for her to escape the reality of today.

Oliver opened his eyes and yawned. Poe smiled weakly. "Good morning."

"Morning. How long you been up?" His voice was deep. Poe had always found his morning voice to be rather enticing even on a day like today.

"For a while."

Oliver turned over on his side. He didn't take his eyes off of her. "Are you okay?" he asked.

No, I'm not okay. Poe sat down on the right side of the bed, facing Oliver. She fidgeted with her hands, then sighed. "I'm scared. I'm afraid after today, I'll lose my happy memories of Jenna. I'm afraid that I'll just remember her in a casket, that's all I'll think." She fought back tears.

Oliver scooted across the bed to grab her hand. "You won't forget those happy times. I promise. A funeral is for you to say goodbye to her."

"I shouldn't have to say goodbye. She should be here. I don't want her gone. It's not fair...it's not fair that she suffered. Jenna got hit by a car; she's probably in a closed casket because she's unrecognizable." She swallowed a knot in her throat. "I can't see my best friend like that. I can't."

Oliver wrapped his arms around Poe. Her tears dampened his t-shirt. She held on to him tightly while he gently rubbed her back. "I promise you, Jenna didn't suffer. She died instantly. I promise you."

She shuddered that he didn't object to a closed casket.

"Poe, look at me."

She thought she'd feel better letting her emotions out, but she just felt worse.

"Look at me, please." Oliver leaned in. "Jenna was happy that day. She came in for breakfast like she did every morning. She was her same goofy self, and she was excited about giving Raven a pink Care Bear. She was laughing and joking with me. She died happy. That's got to count for something, right?"

Poe opened her eyes, glancing at Oliver. Maybe Jenna never saw the car coming. Maybe she was admiring a dress in the window, and it happened so fast that she never felt a thing. Poe made herself believe that Jenna's death was as peaceful as those who die in their sleep.

"A pink Care Bear?" she asked.

"Yeah, one of those gigantic ones."

"Like a body pillow?"

"Yeah. It had a rainbow on its stomach."

"I didn't notice it in Raven's room."

Oliver closed his eyes and squeezed her waist. "Raven never got it. It was stained with blood."

Poe covered her mouth, and held onto Oliver again, resting her head on his chest. She told herself that Jenna died peacefully. There was no blood on the bear. Raven never received it because it was locked away in evidence at the police station. That's what Poe had to believe to make it through the day.

OLIVER SAT AT THE KITCHEN table. His mom walked in, and went straight to the counter, her back to him, pouring herself a cup of coffee. Oliver sighed. He hated the silent treatment. "I'm sorry about last night, Mom."

"What made you change your mind? Or should I ask *who*?"

"I talked to Poe, and she took your side. She helped me understand that my way of dealing with things isn't right for everyone."

"I always said she's a smart girl. Where is she anyway?" His mom turned around and made her way to the table. She sat across from him.

"She's in her room lying down. I'm worried about her." He paused. "She says she can't see Jenna because she thinks she'll look unrecognizable from the accident. She's afraid it'll be a closed casket, and I told her about the Care Bear." He swallowed hard. "Maybe I shouldn't have."

"Shouldn't have what?" Dominic asked, coming in suddenly. Oliver looked down at the table, not knowing how to answer. Today wouldn't be the best time to bring up Jenna's condition. Even though he never said it, Poe was right. That night had been like a scene from a horror movie. There was no need to remind Dominic of that.

"Well, are you going to answer or just sit there?" Dominic took a seat next to Oliver's mom.

'I was just—"

"Just what?"

Oliver's body tensed up. *What's up with everyone always interrupting me? Either they want answers or they don't.*

His mom came to the rescue. "He's worried about Poe because she's afraid to go to the funeral." Oliver didn't want her fighting his battles for him. He felt Dominic's eyes burning through him, but he didn't know why.

"Makes sense," Dominic said. "It'll be her first one. Is that all you were discussing?"

"Pretty much," Lily answered.

"Then what was with Oliver thinking he shouldn't have done that?" Dominic's eyebrow rose. "Done what?"

Before his mom could step in, Oliver said, "I gave her details about the Care Bear. I shouldn't have done that knowing she's already sick to her stomach."

"I should talk to her," Dominic said, but he sounded distant, like he was just going through the motions.

Oliver's mom took a sip of coffee. "It's probably better to give her some space." She rose from her seat and went upstairs.

Oliver caught Dominic glaring at him.

"Hey man, were you two really talking about Poe?" he asked.

"Yeah."

"I thought your mom was just trying to cover for you. I thought you were talking about what happened at my place last night."

"No, I told you I wouldn't."

"I know, but you have to admit you tell your mom everything. I meant what I said. I don't want you telling anybody."

Oliver nodded.

Dominic slapped his hand down on the table. "Well, I better get Raven dressed." He walked away.

Oliver closed his eyes and took a deep breath. After finishing his coffee, he approached the opened door to Poe's bedroom. There was only the unmade bed and empty chair in plain sight. "Poe?"

"In the closet."

He stood at the closet door and watched Poe go through her suitcase. "What are you doing?" He went into panic mode, remembering her flight for tomorrow.

"I should change my shirt. I can't wear this tank top. It's something I would wear to a bar. Besides, it's showing cleavage."

Oliver knelt down beside her. She was wearing a cute, tight pencil skirt, and a black and white striped tank top that supported her double D's perfectly.

"You're beautiful. You don't have to change." He kissed her on the cheek. "If anything, you may want to bring a sweater in case it's too cold in the church."

"I can't believe this is happening. A long time ago, Jenna and I promised each other we'd never miss each other's funeral," Poe whispered, as if talking to herself. "Granted, we thought we'd be in our late nineties or early hundreds."

Oliver rubbed her back, and she leaned into him. He kissed the top of her head. He was grateful that Poe was still opening up to him. That she trusted him. "I have to go home to get ready. Want to come?"

"That's okay. I'll stay here." She didn't even take a second to think about it.

He pouted. It was like one step forward, twenty steps back. She definitely kept him on an emotional rollercoaster, but he'd keep buying ticket after ticket because she was worth it. "Well, maybe I'll see you at the wake."

"I'm only going to the funeral. That's all I can handle. If everyone wants to leave earlier, I'll walk or grab a cab." She frowned. "Unless you need me there."

"No, it's okay. I'm a pallbearer, so I have to sit in a different section. Sit up front, so I can see you." He held her hand. "Okay?"

Poe gave a weak smile. "Okay."

Oliver kissed her on the forehead. "Is there anything I can do for you before I leave?"

"Is there anything I can do for you?" she repeated, staring off into space.

Oliver didn't want to leave her, but he stood up and walked away.

RAVEN SAT ON THE FLOOR while her dad braided her hair. Poe slouched into the cushions of the couch, sitting beside them. Lily sat in the loveseat. Even though the television was on, no one paid attention.

"Be still, Raven. I have to finish. It's almost time for us to go," Dominic said.

"But Mommy always does my hair!"

Poe predicted a temper tantrum coming soon, either from the kid or the dad.

"Well, I'm doing it now."

"But you're not doing it right," Raven said, crossing her arms across her chest.

"You can't see what I'm doing, so you don't know if I'm doing it wrong."

"I can feel it." Raven pouted.

Poe broke into laughter, unable to control herself. Dominic and Lily's staring made the whole situation even sillier.

"Poe, stop laughing at me!" Raven said.

Poe bent over, laughing so hard that she landed on the carpet. She placed her head on Raven's lap. "Raven, I'm not laughing at you; I'm laughing at past events." This was a phrase she and Jenna used to say. Dominic chuckled.

"Whatever you two took this morning, I want some," Lily joked and joined the laughter.

Poe had laughed so hard that she almost peed her pants. In the bathroom, she stood in front of the mirror, looking at her reflection. There were bags under her eyes, and her hair was disheveled. *Am I on the verge of a nervous breakdown?* She sighed. "Please don't laugh at the funeral. Please don't laugh at the funeral. Please don't laugh at the funeral," she repeated, as though she was an obsessive-compulsive person convincing herself not to recheck the stove. With her silliness wearing off, Poe frowned. "Damn you, Jenna, damn you for getting killed."

There was no point stalling anymore. She had to attend the funeral today. Poe convinced herself that she would leave the bathroom after counting to one-hundred.

Through the closed door, she heard Raven scream, "Please don't make me go!"

Poe ran into the living room. Dominic was holding Raven down, while she kicked, screamed, and punched him in the back. Lily was trying to smooth the little girl's hair.

"Please, Daddy. I don't want to go. Please don't make me go." Raven was crying. Each step closer to the front door made her pleas become louder.

"I can't take her like this," Dominic said. "I have no choice but to stay here."

If anyone stays here, it'll be me. "Say goodbye to your wife," Poe said. "I'll stay with her." She walked over and put her hand on Dominic's shoulder.

"But you came all this way to say goodbye. Raven is my responsibility. You do what you planned to do."

"I'll stay with her, Dominic," Poe insisted.

"Raven, is that okay with you?" he asked.

Raven hiccupped. "I wanna stay with Poe."

Dominic hugged his daughter, then let go. He embraced Poe; his black suit felt crisp under her hands. "Thank you," he whispered. "I don't know how I'll ever repay you."

Repay me? "Continue to be my friend unconditionally."

When everyone had gone, Poe massaged Raven's scalp as she settled on her lap. Even though she couldn't see her face, Poe could feel her tears, her shoulder was soaking wet. She rubbed Raven's back while the little diva held on for dear life.

"I want Mommy."

"I know, Raven, I know." Poe closed her eyes, rocking Raven back and forth. Poe didn't know what it felt like to lose a parent. Unfortunately, Raven would learn this tough lesson at a very young age.

Poe couldn't physically bring Jenna into the room, but she hoped she could bring Raven comfort. Still holding Raven, Poe tried to stand on her feet.

"I don't want to go! Please don't make me go!"

"I won't make you do anything you don't want to do. You have to trust me, Raven."

"I trust you, Poe." She sighed, wiping her eyes. Now, Poe was getting somewhere. She wondered what Raven thought about today. Why was she scared to leave with Dominic and Lily?

She carried Raven to the shelf on the wall, where several photos in silver frames were lined up. Poe pointed. "Look, Raven. Look at the pictures."

Raven turned her head to see. "That's Mommy." Poe picked up a frame with Jenna, Oliver, and their cousins, standing in front of a church, wearing formal Easter clothing. They were very young. She showed Raven. "Is that me?" she asked, wide-eyed.

"No, it's your mom when she was around six."

Raven grabbed the photo and held it to her heart. Poe carried her back to the couch and flopped down. Raven sat sideways on her lap.

"I love Mommy and Daddy."

"They love you too."

Raven glanced at her. "Poe, do you love Ollie?"

"Yes." *That was random.* "Do you love me?"

"YES!" Raven wrapped her arms around her neck. Poe laughed softly as they hugged. As long as she could keep her emotions in check, the rest of the morning would run smoothly, except she wouldn't be there for Oliver in case he needed her at the church. Poe bit her bottom lip, knowing she let him down.

Chapter Sixteen

There were many paintings of Jesus on the church's walls, and the maroon seats were so old that dust flew whenever someone sat down. The piano and organ looked antique, like they belonged in the 1920's. The only thing modern inside the building was Jenna's dark blue, shiny casket.

Oliver didn't cry during the funeral. He blocked out the preacher's speeches and prayers, he blocked out his family and friends cries and pleas, and he blocked out all the singing. The louder the preacher got, the more Oliver day-dreamed.

He reminisced about being young and learning about life, when things were good. Oliver thought of kickball, dodgeball, and duck-duck-goose that he and his cousins used to play. He smiled, knowing his grin was probably the only one in the crowd full of frowns.

His mom and Susan, his cousin, were holding Dominic's hands. His mom's body was tense while she looked at the floor, quietly wiping tears from her eyes. Oliver knew she was attempting to be strong for Dominic, whose whole body trembled.

Oliver went through the service like a bad dream.

This can't be happening. He stood at Jenna's gravesite with everyone else. Her casket was suspended over an open hole, draped with artificial green turf. Baskets of flowers and wreaths surrounded the blue tent.

Everything was so permanent, so final. He'd never see Jenna again. Oliver thought of the others who were buried in that graveyard. He looked down at his feet, then at everyone else's. Were they stepping on top of someone? Would a stranger step on Jenna, not caring who she was?

It fascinated Oliver how people could become so narrow-minded when they lost a loved one; that they only focused on that person's tombstone. But, it was a community—a dead community. Jenna would be buried near her third cousins. Hopefully, they would take care of her and show her the ropes of the graveyard. Maybe she'd come back as a ghost and haunt the place. She had always loved to scare people.

The preacher ended his farewell, and people began to walk away, but Oliver didn't budge. He needed to stay with his cousin. He cried silently to himself; no sound escaped his lips. He covered his mouth with his hand. An arm rested on Oliver's shoulders, leading him away. He didn't bother looking to see who the person was.

"You lucky bastard," a voice said. "You got a full view of all the boobies. I know you were smiling because of Sam's knockers." His cousin Bradley. Of course, today didn't affect him. He was too self-centered. "Damn, if she wears a skin tight mini to church, I can only imagine what she wears to clubs. I should've visited Jenna at work more often." Bradley changed direction to make them head sideways instead of straight towards the vehicles. "Cuz, be my wingman. I've been trying to get with the Shannon twins since high school."

Bradley stopped. Oliver uncovered his face to see his neighbor Melinda and her twin Belinda in front of them. They greeted each other with hugs, but Bradley held on to the women a bit longer than expected. Oliver was surprised that he didn't try to feel them up.

"Hello, lovely ladies," Bradley flirted. Melinda blushed, looking down to the ground.

"Why weren't you a pallbearer?" Belinda asked.

"Look at me. Would you want me to drop the casket?" He was scrawny, and his suit looked baggy on him. He had brown curly hair and brown eyes. Bradley laughed while Belinda stifled a giggle. He walked over to her and placed his arm around her shoulders. She must be the bait. Bradley didn't need a wingman because he could handle things on his own.

"Here comes your girl." Bradley smirked. The twins frowned. Oliver turned around hoping to see Poe, but it was Kate heading towards them. *She won't show off at a funeral, will she?*

"Gotta go; come on, Melinda." The twins speed-walked away. Kate watched them—if looks could kill.

"Cuz, I'd run after them, but I have a feeling you'll need my help." Bradley gave a wide grin as Kate reached them. She folded her arms across her chest and stared at Oliver, who looked at his cousin. "Those chicks were for me, but if you give me a chance, I'll totally dump them. Oliver's your Dawson. I can be your Pacey."

If Oliver was in a better mood, he would have laughed. Ever since they were pre-teens, Bradley watched movies and television shows that were popular with females in the hopes that it would improve his game; that girls would find him sensitive and let their guard down. It was funny because girls saw through the bullshit, the smart ones anyway.

"What are you doing here?" Oliver asked.

"I came to pay my respects, but it looks like you're fine. The first instinct after burying Jenna is to flirt with those ugly bitches? That's awesome." Kate rolled her eyes. "I knew that bitch always liked you—patting you on the back yesterday, now giving you a hug."

Bradley looked like a wounded puppy. "Did you not hear me? Those two were for me."

"Can you leave us alone? I want to talk to Oliver," she snapped.

"No, don't leave," Oliver said. "Whatever you have to say, you can say in front of him." If Kate didn't have an attitude, he would talk alone, but not when she's in a mood like this. He couldn't deal with that right now. There was no way he was participating in a scene in front of his family and friends.

Bradley's head went back and forth like a ping pong.

Kate's cheeks were bright red. "I can't get alone time with you?"

Oliver sighed. "What do you want, Kate?"

"I want you to say you made a mistake and come back to me. I'm here for you." Kate scanned the cemetery. "Poe clearly isn't. She couldn't even bother to attend her so-called best friend's funeral. I knew that wasn't her real reason for showing up. She just wanted to take you from me."

"Wait. Poe's here?" Bradley interrupted. "And I'm just finding this out now? Why didn't you tell me, Cuz?"

"You're wrong about Poe." Oliver frowned. "I'm sorry, but you have to move on."

"You can move on to me." Bradley grinned. "We can have some good revenge, rebound sex. That would make Cuz jealous. If not, a plus would be you kept it in the MacNamara family."

"Shut up, Bradley. I've always hated you."

"Hate is a strong word. I think you try to convince yourself that because you're actually in love with me. You can't resist my hotness and charm. No lady can, really."

Bradley could talk in circles forever and a day, but Oliver didn't have time for that. The sooner he could end this conversation, the sooner he could find Poe. "I really appreciate you paying your respects. It really means a lot, more than you'll ever know, but I really have to go. Bye, Kate." He turned to walk away with his cousin following him.

"Don't walk away from me!"

Bradley turned his head. "Get a clue. Cuz doesn't want you anymore, but you can still call me." He smirked.

OLIVER DROVE WHILE Bradley messed with the radio buttons. "You're too nice, Cuz. You should've told Kate to shut up. Don't let anyone disrespect you."

"She wants drama. That's why I don't give it to her."

"Well, you better watch your back. I don't think Ms. Psycho takes no for an answer; if I find you gutted behind some bushes, I'll know who to suspect."

Oliver gave him a quick glance. He considered Kate's drama queen threats harmless, but what if she was really crazy? "I could take her."

"I don't know. Crazies have the power to overtake their opponents. You need to watch some scary movies to see what I'm talking about. Seen any boiling bunnies lately?"

"Huh?"

"Exactly." Bradley smacked his forehead and gave Oliver a disappointed stare. He leaned back in his seat. "Now, when did Poe get here?"

"Monday. She's been staying at my mom's."

"What the hell? Once again, why wasn't I told? I would've been there in the quickness."

It takes two to communicate, and Oliver didn't remember getting any phone calls from Bradley. So, he had no room to talk. "Would've been wasting your time. I've been staying there too." Oliver shook his head. "And, Kate's wrong. Poe didn't come back for me; she came for Jenna's funeral, but Mom told me she couldn't make it because Raven was crying hysterically, too afraid to come, so Poe stayed to calm her down and to give Dominic the chance to come." His eyes left the road for a split second, so he could glance over at his cousin. "And that's why I'm in love with Poe."

"And that's why I'm in love with her too."

Deep down, Oliver figured that was probably true. While Jenna had attended WVU, Bradley always visited her in Morgantown, and when he came home, he would talk about his crush on Jenna's roommate. Since Bradley tried to get in every woman's pants, Oliver never took his cousin seriously. When Poe moved to Providence, Oliver pursued her. Bradley had given him the silent treatment for about a month, and his cousin *loved* to talk. Oliver apologized, but he couldn't help how he felt about Poe. Of course, he wouldn't have made a move if she would've shown any romantic interest towards Bradley whatsoever. On the other hand, maybe he would have. People can't help who they fall in love with.

Out of revenge, Bradley had hooked up with one of Oliver's exes. Douche bag.

Oliver tried to change the subject. "Won't the person you drove with wonder where you are?"

"Nah, I rode with Sis. She has to take Baby Niece to a dance recital. There's no way I'm going to that. I'm hungry. I want to be one of the first people at the reception. That's why I pulled you away, but I have a feeling you're going to go find Poe." He raised his left and right palms like a balance scale. "Poe. Food. Poe. Food." He smiled. "I pick Poe too. A win-win."

Did Bradley ever listen to himself speak? Oliver knew his motive would reveal itself—wanting to stay and help, his ass.

Chapter Seventeen

Drawings and colored pencils were spread all over the couch; some had even fallen to the floor. Poe's mini-sketchbook was open on the coffee table with pages—scribbles all over—torn from it. Poe had volunteered to sketch Raven whatever she wanted, but the little diva had insisted she draw Poe something instead. Poe was flattered and decided she'd hang the pictures up on her walls when she got back to her apartment in Pittsburgh. Whenever anyone would ask her about them, she would always remember this bonding moment with Raven.

Poe never thought she'd be able to share anything meaningful with a kid. It's not that she didn't like children, she was just scared. Maybe kids were like dogs and could smell fear? These past couple of days showed her that she had a lot to offer, so she should experiment being closer to kids, learning about them, possibly being a baby-sitter once in a while for her friends, or hanging out with her niece more often.

Hearing the front door open, Poe assumed that it was Lily checking in on things before work. She glanced over at the clock on the wall; it read 12:30. Raven ran into the kitchen. "Ollie! Bradie!"

Poe ran her hand through her hair. *Will Oliver be upset or disappointed with me?* He had made such a fuss about how his mom would spend today. Maybe he wouldn't approve of her choice either.

Raven jumped up into Oliver's arms as he walked around the corner with Bradley. Both resembled GQ models. Poe crossed the room in anticipation of an embrace from Oliver. They locked gazes as she fought back tears. "Sorry I missed it."

"It's okay." Hesitantly, he released one arm from her back. She studied his eyes for any hint of lying or disapproval, and sighed in relief.

Bradley grabbed Poe's hand and spun her around to face him. "Can I have a hug?" Without waiting for her response, he wrapped his arms around her. "I see you saved the best for last," he whispered in her ear, his breath tickling the side of her face. She tried to back away, but he held on for three seconds longer.

Even though Bradley acted like a nuisance sometimes, Poe found him charming and endearing. She didn't have a crush on him, but she loved the attention he gave her. Bradley was a player while Oliver was sincere. That's why she would never fall for Bradley's charm. She shook her head, figuring he probably made an ass out of himself during the funeral service. If he was anywhere near Oliver or Dominic, he probably didn't allow them space to grieve properly.

"I'm hungry," Raven said.

Bradley playfully punched Oliver's arm. "Come on, Cuz. Let's go to the reception."

"Reception?" Raven asked.

"Yeah, Baby Cuz, it's where your dad is at."

Raven gripped onto Oliver's back and wrapped her legs around his waist in a frantic way. "Please don't make me go!"

"It's okay." He patted her back, a thin line formed on his lips. "We'll eat somewhere else."

Poe frowned. Comforting Dominic would have to wait.

IN THE CAR, BRADLEY messed with the radio buttons. Every five seconds, he turned the station, so a song couldn't finish. By the time he decided on something he liked, it was already over, forcing him to fast forward through commercial breaks. He'd start all over again, which interrupted Poe's train of thought while she glanced out the window.

Raven pointed and folded her arms across her chest. "Bradie, stop—stop that."

He shrugged his shoulders. "Stop what?"

"Leave it on a song," Raven demanded.

"No, I like to hear all my options first before making a decision."

"Have you ever noticed that when you finally make a decision, the song is long gone?" Oliver asked, tapping his fingers impatiently on the steering wheel.

"Exactly. That's why I have to start over." Bradley changed the station again.

"BRADIE, STOP IT!"

"I said no."

Not again. Poe couldn't take another drawn out argument in Oliver's car. Was his car cursed? She shook her head and sighed. It'd be a long ride to IHOP. "Raven, is it bugging you that much? If so, you'll get way more by being nice about it instead of being bossy." Or a diva.

"Okay, Poe." Raven sighed, her eyes wide with hope. "Please stop it. Please—please leave it on a song."

Bradley smirked. "No."

Raven huffed and puffed; she looked at Poe with frustration in her eyes.

Poe scooted up and tapped him on the shoulder. He turned to face her. Their heads were only inches apart. "Come on, Bradley, she just lost her mom. Give her a break, just this once," she whispered in his ear.

"Only if you kiss me."

Poe rolled her eyes, sneered, then slapped his shoulder. How could he be a jerk to his little cousin? There was self-centered, and there was being a giant douche bag. She couldn't believe him right now.

"No, Bradie. You and Poe can't kiss. Don't hurt Ollie." Raven balled her left hand up in a fist and was attempting to unbuckle her seat belt. Poe touched her arm, trying to get her to calm down. Her main priority was making sure Raven was safe.

Poe scolded herself for setting a bad example—violence was never the answer. "Don't pay him any mind. Just give him the side eye."

Bradley laughed while Oliver's hands gripped tighter on the steering wheel. Soon Poe would have to calm him down too. If she ignored everyone, maybe the problem would go away. No. In the past, she would've used her gift of tuning people out, but not anymore. No more running away from issues.

"There's no need for that ladies. I'm sorry. I can't bear having my two favorite girls mad at me." Bradley slumped back into his seat and didn't touch anything for the rest of the ride.

Raven smirked.

IN IHOP, THE GROUP sat in the center of the room. Oliver sat beside Raven, and Bradley sat near Poe. Most of the tables were full of elderly couples and parents with their children.

"If I would've known you were here sooner, I would've visited. When do you leave?" Bradley asked Poe.

"When I fall asleep tonight, it'll be Thursday. That's when Poe leaves," Raven explained, not looking up from her paper mat she was coloring with a red crayon.

"Damn, that soon. Well, so much for giving you and Cuz alone time tonight. I'm staying the third wheel." He winked at Oliver. "Then tomorrow I can give you a ride to the airport."

Oliver chuckled condescendingly. "You need a license first."

"Correction." Bradley grinned as he moved his chair closer to Poe's seat. "I'll find a ride to the airport."

Who does Bradley think he is, flirting with Poe right in front of my face? Oliver trusted Poe, but he didn't trust his cousin, since Bradley had already slept with one of his exes. Apparently, Leo wasn't his only competition. He folded his arms across his chest, glaring at Bradley. He knew Poe didn't like displays of jealousy, so he wanted to keep his emotions in check.

"I'm sure your girlfriend would mind that," Poe said. Bradley had someone in his life, who gave birth to two of his children. Not officially a couple, he hooked up with her when he went to visit his one and two-year olds, or when he went to pay child support. Other than that, Bradley didn't care what she did, but she certainly cared what he was up to. Oliver would never treat the mother of his children like that. He wished Bradley had more respect for women; he gave the MacNamara men a bad rep.

"That's why I'm smart enough to never date a girl from Smith Hill." Bradley ran his hands through his hair. He tapped his fork on his glass of Mountain Dew, creating an upbeat rhythm. "If she wants to act out, she can keep that shit in her own neighborhood."

Poe shook her head, suppressing a giggle. Oliver sighed and leaned into his seat. *Why can't she see through his bullshit? Why doesn't she ever cuss him out or ignore him?* "You see, there's this thing called a car."

"Oh thanks, Cuz. You think I'm worth using gas on. Thanks so much."

Oliver rolled his eyes and rubbed his chin roughly.

The waitress arrived at their table and set the plates of food in front of them. "Thanks, beautiful." Bradley winked seductively. She walked away, smiling and blushing. "Works every time." There were more strips of bacon and an extra pancake on his plate.

Oliver cut Raven's pancakes. She raved about the delicious food, then she and Bradley discussed their favorite Disney shows, which led to his venting about missing *Hannah Montana*. Poe laughed as Bradley was getting more passionate. Guess they got over their rift in the car.

Oliver looked down at his plate and gulped down his eggs. A knot formed in his throat, so he drank a sip of coffee. Seconds later, Poe rubbed her foot up and down his leg. He lifted his head to grin at her. His heart raced. Poe smiled.

Oliver almost wished there were less laughs and less smiles today. It seemed like no one cared about Jenna. He wanted to snap out of his funk because he didn't want Poe's last night to be spent with him this way. He also hated having to share Poe with everyone. Yes, life went on, but it didn't have to be rushed the day Jenna was buried.

Poe joined the conversation. "You know a show that I really miss. I really miss *Greek*."

"Yeah, Ashley was hot," Bradley said. "Oliver's your Evan while I'm your Cappie."

Poe gazed into Oliver's eyes. "No, he's my Rusty. My sweet, smart, sexy Rusty." Oliver smiled, though he had no idea who those guys were.

Bradley blew the waitress a kiss when she laid the check on the table. "Thanks, beautiful."

During their lunch, the waitress had stopped by their table four times, which Oliver considered a record. Whenever he dined in a restaurant alone, he could hardly get anyone to come fill up his drink.

She walked to his side of the table and handed him a piece of paper. "Here's my phone number, handsome." They looked each other up and down from head to toe, as though they were auditioning for a porno.

Poe and Oliver shared a glance.

Bradley watched his future hook-up leave, skimmed over the bill, then handed it to Oliver. "I need to use the bathroom."

"Me too," Raven said. They got up from the table and walked, holding hands, to the back of the restaurant.

Oliver shook his head. "Typical Bradley, always running out on the bill." It was time to follow his advice of getting out of his funky mood, he scolded himself. Finally, alone time. He shouldn't waste it talking about his cousin's shortcomings.

Poe opened her purse and pulled out some one-dollar bills.

"No, I got it."

"My money's not counterfeit, remember?" Poe joked.

Yes, he remembered. Their argument yesterday was still a fresh wound. "I seem to recall you saying I'm too nice. Bradley said that to me in the car too. What does that even mean?" He placed a five-dollar bill and some ones under his plate.

They strolled to the counter with their arms intertwined. "The time you take focusing on other people feeling better,' she said. "You should devote some of that time making yourself feel better."

Oliver couldn't help it; he was happy when his company was happy. Even as a little boy, he had always tried to please everyone, especially adults. After he paid the bill, they waited outside on the sidewalk near a blue bench. They stood so close he could feel her body heat. His head tilted to the side.

Poe's left hand held on to the bottom of his shirt, rubbing against his belt buckle, teasing his senses. She searched his eyes. "Are you okay?"

He frowned. "I miss Jenna."

"Me too." She closed her eyes, sighing.

"And, I feel bad that I wasn't with you this morning. I should have been there."

"Don't worry about me."

"You're all I worry about."

Chapter Eighteen

After IHOP, they dropped Raven off with Dominic. Poe had offered to watch her again, but he wanted to be near his daughter. Plus, no one wanted to wake her up from her nap; she looked peaceful in bed. Oliver, Bradley, and Poe had spent an hour comforting Dominic—for Bradley, it was more like showing off. Then, Oliver brought Bradley back to his apartment even though he didn't want to. His cousin had promised that he would hang out with the Shannon twins.

Yeah right.

It was 8:30 PM, and he was still there, relaxed on the couch with his feet propped on the coffee table. "Thanks for the dinner, Cuz."

"No problem, but if you really want to thank me, you can wash the dishes."

Bradley smirked. Oliver rolled his eyes.

"I'll help you, Oliver," Poe said, hitting Bradley on the arm. He grabbed her hand, leaned over her, and trapped her in her space on the couch. "No, you have to stay and keep me company. Pretty please."

That's all it took for Poe to change her mind. Oliver glared, gathered the plates, then went into the kitchen. The room was connected to the living room, so he could see everything. He hardly paid attention to scrubbing. He figured he'd have to re-clean the dishes later.

When Oliver entered the living room again, Bradley managed to weasel himself closer to Poe. He touched her knee whenever the show amused him, and she didn't seem uncomfortable with it. Their eyes were glued to the television set.

Oliver sat in his loveseat and rubbed his forehead. Another headache was on its way. "Come on, Bradley, you have to go. Do you need me to take you, or can you get a ride?"

"Nah, Cuz. I'm not leaving."

"Brad—"

"Nah, come on now. I'm watching TV. I need to see who wins POV."

"Screw POV. I'll knock my TV off the wall, then you can't see anything."

"What's your problem, Cuz? Can't you chill somewhere else? You're bothering us, and I *know* you don't want to bother Poe." He seemed amused.

Poe stood up and sat sideways on Oliver's lap, wrapped her arms around his chest, and rested her head on his shoulder. "Babe, it's against the law to make someone miss *Big Brother*. We've got to see who wins POV. Please be Brenden, someone needs to break up the Brigade."

Oliver rubbed her back and stared at the television set. POV? *Big Brother?* Brigade? It was as if she was speaking a foreign language, and he needed Rosetta Stone to comprehend. He would never succeed in getting his cousin out if he couldn't even get her on his side. He rolled his eyes.

During a commercial break, Bradley asked, "Cuz, can you get me a soda?"

'No, but you can get it yourself."

"Poe, be a darling and ask him to get a soda." He waved his hand dismissively. "He'll get up for you, then you can give it to me."

"No. Get it yourself," she said. Oliver and Poe gave each other a high five. Maybe they could get on the same page after all. Bradley flipped them the bird, rose from the couch, then kicked Oliver in the foot when he passed. "I can see you're not a southern gentleman."

"Now that you realize it, I don't have to be nice anymore." Oliver tickled Poe. She kicked her feet. When she grabbed his hands, he leaned down to kiss her. Her hands caressed his face while they kissed. He held on to her waist, trying to slip her skirt down.

They didn't realize Bradley had entered the room until he popped his soda can. Poe pulled away from Oliver's lips and placed her head on his chest. Oliver, with sweat dripping from his forehead, breathed heavily.

Damn it, Bradley!

Bradley plopped down in his seat. "You lucky bastard. You get front row seats to Sam's double D's. You have your recent ex sweating you while your other ex takes you back. All three very hot. If this happened to me, somehow I'd be an asshole. But, of course, you get away with it. Please tell me how you do it."

"Sam's double D's?" Poe asked, releasing her grip from Oliver's waist. Her entire body tensed. "You mean the girl Jenna worked with?"

"Yeah. She had on this tight black mini like she was looking to make some extra bucks." Bradley winked at Poe. "Your man was looking. You should have seen how hard he was grinning."

"I wasn't grinning," Oliver said through clenched teeth.

Bradley smirked. "Like hell you weren't."

"I didn't even notice Sam. I was thinking about when we were all kids." He glared at Bradley. "Don't sit there and try to cause trouble."

"I'm not causing trouble—just stating facts." Bradley shook his head while making eye contact with Poe. "Like the fact Kate approached Cuz after the funeral, wanting him back and questioning why you weren't there."

Poe shot up from Oliver's lap, her back facing him. He couldn't believe Bradley was doing this. He took cockblocking to a whole different level. Oliver prayed that Poe wouldn't take the bait.

She spun around, her hands on her hips. "Did you talk to her?"

"Poe, no. I didn't." He averted his gaze to the floor then back to her brown eyes, his eyes pleading. "I mean—"

"You should've talked to her," she said.

"I know, right." Bradley's eyes were focused on Oliver. "I had his back from her jealousy only to be kicked in the balls with new information that they aren't even together anymore. That he's shacked up with you. No wonder Kate is stalking his ass. Poe's right—you should've talked to her instead of sticking your tail between your legs."

Oliver couldn't look at his cousin. He gripped the armrests of the loveseat. "What do you mean I should've talked to her?"

"She was there to talk to you. It would've been nice to give her the time of day. Clearly, Kate's not over you, and I don't blame her. It's fine if you don't want to get back together, but the decent thing to do is give her time to adjust. At least give Kate closure."

"Poe, if it means that much to you, I'll talk to her."

"It shouldn't matter what I think. You should do it because you were in a relationship with her. Because at one time she was your one and only. That's why you should do it, Oliver." Poe walked into the bedroom and slammed the door.

Bradley grinned, eyes set on the show again. "If you guys have make-up sex, can I watch?"

"GET THE FUCK OUT, BRADLEY!" Oliver shot up, grabbed his cousin by the arm, lifted him up from the couch, and pushed him backwards toward the front door.

"Wait, wait." Bradley frowned, stumbling, holding onto Oliver's arm so he wouldn't fall down. "Let me make things right. I'll go talk to her and smooth things over."

"No, I'll smooth things over myself." Oliver took a deep breath. His heart beat slowed down. "Do you need money?"

"Nah, but thanks for asking. That's the Cuz I know." Bradley opened the door and left.

Chapter Nineteen

Poe fanned herself after making love, the breeze cooled off Oliver's hot, sweaty body. "When I came here, I knew I'd end up in a hotel. I really thought I'd take all week to work on my comic in my room alone, or spend more of my time with Dominic. I thought I'd only see you at the funeral."

Oliver ran his fingertips over the pulse of Poe's neck, and he raised his chin, his soft lips taking in the warmth of her skin there, eager to kiss but too exhausted to bite. "No way, I would've found you at the hotel."

"You could've found me, but it doesn't mean I'd open the door," she teased.

"I'd kick it open." He tried to regain his strength in case she wanted to go for round two. Apparently, she had a lot of energy left.

When Bradley left, Oliver had eased all of Poe's fears away. He reassured her that he hadn't talked to Kate because he thought she was there to cause trouble. The day he met Poe and Raven at the pier, Oliver had already told Kate that he was in love with Poe. And he explained why he never asked her why she didn't attend the funeral. She thought he had expected her to find an excuse, so he wasn't surprised. Instead, his reason was that his mom had already told him at the wake. Oliver's honesty caused Poe to open up to him. Their heart to heart led to lovemaking.

Poe sighed. "It's so crazy that I'm back here. Next month, Jenna, Dominic, and Raven were supposed to visit me. I was going to show them Kennyworld." She frowned and held back tears. "Now it won't happen. I mean, Dominic and Raven can still come, but it won't be the same without her...Do you think Dominic will be okay?"

Oliver sighed, sharing a glance with his one true love. He kissed her cheek, then rolled over to the left side of the bed. He lay on his side with his head resting on his arms. "I hope so, but I honestly don't know. It's too early to tell."

Poe yawned. Maybe she didn't have any more energy after all. She caressed his cheek, and he took the opportunity to kiss her hand. They started to discuss having a long distance relationship, but Poe dozed off. Oliver nudged her.

"You should get some sleep," she said. "You've got to get up early tomorrow."

"I don't care. I'd rather stay up and talk to you. Did you tell Leo about us?" It was now or never for the truth. She was adamant that he talk to Kate. Well, did she follow her own advice and woman up to Leo?

She backed away from Oliver, still facing him. His arm fell from her back and landed on the sheets. "It's not exactly a conversation to have over the phone."

"But you will tell him?"

"Yes," she hesitated. "I should."

Oliver scooted closer, placing his arm around the middle of her back again. Poe gave him a quick peck on the lips. "You should stay...I know you wanted to be here until the weekend, and you can. On Saturday, I can drive you home. You'll get there before Monday morning."

"Tomorrow is your first day back." Poe backed away again. "I can't ask you to call off the weekend too."

"I don't care about that. I want to spend more time with you, so my boss will just have to understand that." A ten-hour road trip would be the perfect opportunity for them to continue reconnecting again.

"Oliver—"

"Before you say no, please think about it."

Poe rose out of bed, bent down, and threw on her underwear and tank top that were lying on the floor. Without saying a word, she walked out of the bedroom.

Oliver frowned. He had pushed too hard, and now she would distance herself again. He waited to see if Poe would come back to bed. His heart ached. After a little while, he put on his boxers and left.

Since it was dark in the hallway, Oliver switched on the light. He heard Poe's voice barely above a whisper in the living room. *Who is she talking to this late at night?*

Before he approached her, Poe hung up her cell phone. She sat on the couch, rubbing her foot. "I stubbed my toe on your couch. All these bruises that I have, Mom will think you guys beat me up while I was here."

Oliver dropped to his knees and kissed her big toe, then lifted her shirt to kiss her stomach. He held her hand and kissed her finger. "Feel better?" he asked, looking at her.

"Yes."

Oliver closed his eyes. "Poe, please think about what I said."

"I don't have to think about anything, Oliver." She caressed his face.

"Poe—"

"I don't have to think about it because I just got finished canceling my ticket."

It took a second for him to absorb the information. He smiled and placed his head on Poe's lap. He felt elated. She was fighting for them as well. He lay down behind her on the couch, both of them turning sideways to fit. He wrapped his arm around her.

"I love you, Oliver."

His eyes glistened with happiness. They would be okay. They would make it. "I love you too."

"Do you love me enough to let me sleep?"

They laughed.

Chapter Twenty

Oliver counted to ten before going into the restaurant where he worked. On the count of six, he stood out of the way and opened the door for a joyful couple walking past. "Five, four, three, two...one." He took a deep breath and went through the front door. He smiled at the hostess; she waved.

The thirty-table room was crowded with customers. One day a foodie had blogged that Four Leaf Clover had the best breakfast in town, and after that, the restaurant was crowded every morning. Tommy, the owner, decided to make breakfast an option throughout the entire day. Business boomed ever since.

Oliver felt eyes from every table watching him, as if he was a puzzle they needed to solve. He tugged at his chef's jacket. When he reached the owner's office, the door was open, so he stood in the doorway. Tommy was on the phone but acknowledged Oliver's presence by wiggling his finger. Oliver stepped inside and waited patiently.

Tommy had given Oliver a job at a young age, and in a way, Oliver had looked up to him as a dad even though he knew he could never take James's place in Tommy's heart.

"Hey let me call you back...okay bye."

Oliver stuffed his hands in his pockets. "You didn't have to hang up on my account."

"Yes I did, Chef."

Oliver wished he would call him by his name. Tommy had explained a long time ago that it was a respect thing, which he would understand if he had gone to culinary school. Out of respect, Oliver wanted to call him Mr. Farrell, but Tommy wouldn't allow it.

"How are you?" Tommy asked.

"I'll be fine."

"And your mom?"

"I think she's holding up better than me to tell you the truth."

"Yeah, well Lily has always been a strong woman." He grabbed an envelope off his desk and handed it to Oliver. "This is from all of us at Four Leaf Clover."

He slid his finger under the flap and pulled out a sympathy card. Tommy, the manager, waiters, hostesses, busboys, and the cooks wrote personalized remarks, saying how sorry they were for Oliver's loss. He covered his mouth, tears fell involuntary down his face. His body trembled. Tommy closed the door, then patted him on the back.

"Thank you. This means so much," Oliver said between sniffs. "Sorry."

"Chef, it's all right. Do you need more time off? It's okay if you do; your sous chef has done a great job running the kitchen, and I think he likes the overtime. Needs all the money he can get since his girlfriend is expecting."

"No, I can do this. I just need a minute." Oliver took a deep breath. Tommy sat down at his desk. "Thanks again." He lifted the card, then placed his hand on the doorknob. Oliver turned to face Tommy. *I have nothing to lose.* They stared at each other. "Do you know where my dad is?"

Tommy lowered his head and fidgeted with his hands. "Does Lily know you're asking about him?"

"No, and I'd like to keep it that way, at least until I'm ready to tell her."

"What's making you ask now?"

"Do you want me to get to work, or do you want to be my therapist all day? If you pick option B, I'll gladly pull up a chair and pour my heart and soul on the table. May involve some crying, so be ready for it."

Tommy sighed. "He's my best friend, but he's dumber than a box of rocks for leaving you and Lily. Only John would leave Providence to go live in a swamp. He gives crocodile tours in the Everglades."

"Does he have any kids?"

"Nah, John never wanted kids." He covered his mouth. "Sorry, I didn't mean—"

"No, it's okay. I get it." He flinched. Maybe his mom had lied about his dad always playing games with him and showing him love, support, and affection. His dad probably never gave him the time of day.

Now, everything made sense. He left shortly after Jenna moved in, so Oliver figured his dad couldn't take one, definitely not two, kids at a time. It's not like Jenna asked for both of her parents to die, leaving her an orphan.

Fuck John Smith.

Oliver spent twenty-four years without him, so he would continue to do so. "I guess I've been thinking about him lately because I miss Jenna. It opened the doors to other people, who were missing in my life, but some should stay that way."

"Oliver, I'm sorry."

"No, don't be. You've been a better father figure than he'll ever be. I should get to work." Oliver opened the door and left. He shut it, leaning up against the cold steel.

LILY AND POE SAT AT a table facing the window. The hot chocolate, coffee, and baked pastries were paradise to Poe's nostrils. She was mad at herself for not coming to her favorite café earlier in the week.

Lily grinned. "You want me," she teased. "That's the real reason you left my son last year."

"I've kept my feelings hidden for so long." Poe placed her hand over her heart. "Thank goodness, you finally figured it out. Thank goodness."

Both women burst out laughing.

"Don't tell, Oliver," Poe said.

"Never. We'll just keep our love a secret."

"Oh, so my love is reciprocated." Poe winked.

Lily nodded, and Poe imitated Raven by clapping. "But no seriously," Lily said. "Oliver took it pretty hard when you left; it was like he shut down, which I never guessed he would do. He's always been an open book. Since you came back, I see the spark in him again. I want my son to be happy, and he's happy with you."

"I asked him if he wanted a long distance relationship."

"Oh no, hon. You two can't do that; you have to be near each other. I wasn't going to say anything, but I think you should know that Jenna confided in me that they had a plan for him to move to Pittsburgh to woo you back."

Move to Pittsburgh? Poe never heard that from anyone, so Lily must be mistaken. Before she could respond, Lily placed her hand on top of Poe's hand.

"I've always thought of you as a daughter. Now, it's time to make it official, Poe MacNamara."

"Or, he can be called Oliver Allen."

"Since you're talking about it instead of changing the subject, I take it it's something you may consider." Lily smiled.

Poe could not believe Oliver would move without her knowledge. She took a deep breath. "Lily, do you want grandchildren?"

"I want my son to be happy."

Poe took another sip of coffee, looking out the window. She noticed the people walking on the sidewalk outside. They were living their normal lives, like Jenna had on Sunday. A man, talking on his cell phone, stood in front of the window, peering inside. Then, he strolled away. Poe thought of Jenna stopping in front of a shop window. She wiped a tear.

"I'm sorry, hon. I didn't mean to make you upset."

Poe blurted, "Jenna hates me. We made a pact in college that when one of us dies, the other has to go to the funeral to say goodbye. I didn't, so she hates me now." Poe slouched and looked at the floor.

"Jenna doesn't hate you. She can't hate you because she can't feel anything. She's dead. No one is mad that you missed it, so you shouldn't feel bad...you can say goodbye at Jenna's gravesite. Win—win."

Poe rubbed the rim of her coffee cup. Lily continued, "Jenna's biggest fear was being gone from her children at a young age where they couldn't remember her. It sucks that her nightmare came true. Raven will forget all about her just like Jenna had done with her parents." Lily looked down at the table and took her hand off Poe's. She put her hand over her mouth and closed her eyes.

Poe wiped another tear and looked at Lily. She didn't know what to say. She appreciated seeing this side of Lily; it made her feel special like she found a hidden key to a magical box.

"It's 2010, you know," Lily said. "Women can propose to men now."

"You think Oliver would go for that?"

"My son is old-fashioned, but he won't propose unless he was absolutely, positively sure you would say yes, so I don't see him asking anytime soon." Lily grinned and winked. "So, you should make the first move."

"Tell me how you really feel."

"I just did, but I don't mind repeating it again."

Poe smiled, sitting up in her seat. "Are you serious that Oliver was moving to Pittsburgh?"

"Yes. Jenna told me that she, Dominic, and Raven were visiting you next month. Oliver was going to tag along to look for a place to stay and work, then maybe in a month or two, he'd officially move. Oliver should do it sooner, but he feels obligated to Tommy and Four Leaf Clover."

In the parking lot, Poe stood beside Lily's 1980 red Mustang.

"Are you sure you don't need a ride?" Lily asked, getting in.

"I'm sure. I'll just walk to the pier," Poe lied. It was right across the street, but she did not intend to go there. She watched Lily drive off, then walked three blocks to the boutique where Jenna was killed. Caution tape was wrapped around the building, and there was heavy duty tape covering the hole where a glass window once was. On the sidewalk, there was a blue cross with flowers.

Poe took a deep breath and approached the building, her back turned to the traffic in the street and pedestrians on the sidewalk. She covered her mouth and tuned out the noise of people walking, cars driving, and birds tweeting.

She closed her eyes. If she could, Poe would take her best friend's place in the coffin. She began breathing faster and closed her eyes tighter. *Please run over me.* She waited for a car to hit her, but none ever did.

She sighed, opening her eyes, and stood in silence for a while. She sat on the sidewalk, facing the street. She watched people and cars go by. She felt the sun beat on her shoulders and smelled the ocean breeze. She couldn't take Jenna's place, so she would live her life the best way she knew how.

She dialed Dominic's number. "Hello?" he said.

"Hey, Dominic. Do you and Raven want to eat breakfast with me at Four Leaf Clover?"

Poe had a life-changing question she needed to ask Oliver.

THE END

About the Author

Yawatta Hosby resides in the eastern panhandle of West Virginia. She teaches creative writing through the Adult Community Education program, and she enjoys connecting with other writers through blogging. With a desire to escape every day life, she creates short stories, novellas, and novels. She's always had a fascination with psychology, so she likes to focus on the inner-struggles within her characters. Yawatta is also an avid reader, favorite genres: mystery, thriller, horror, and women's fiction.

She'd love to hear from her fans and readers:

Blog: http://yawattahosby.wordpress.com[1]

Twitter: http://www.twitter.com/yawatta_hosby

Author Page on Facebook: http://www.facebook.com/YawattaHosby

---

1.   http://yawattahosby.wordpress.com/

Other Stories by Author

O NE BY ONE (Mystery Thriller/Horror)

FOR A COMPLETE LISTING of Yawatta Hosby's books and free short stories, please visit her author website: http://yawattahosbysbooks.word-press.com[1]

---

1. http://yawattahosbysbooks.wordpress.com/

Don't miss out!

Visit the website below and you can sign up to receive emails whenever Yawatta Hosby publishes a new book. There's no charge and no obligation.

https://books2read.com/r/B-A-LFIB-CNCX

BOOKS 2 READ

Connecting independent readers to independent writers.

Also by Yawatta Hosby

One By One
Something's Amiss
Twisted Obsession
Six Plus One
Perfect Little Murder
Two Book Boxset
Urban Legends

Watch for more at yawattahosbysbooks.wordp.